D1588259

I'LL TELL YOU A STORY

by

ENID BLYTON

Illustrated by Eileen A. Soper

MACMILLAN AND CO. LIMITED
ST. MARTIN'S STREET, LONDON
1943

CONTENTS

THE PEPPERMINT PARTY

OUTSIDE the nursery, under the lilac bush, there lived Twink and Topple, two small brownies. They made peppermint cakes for their living, and they were so delicious that all the pixies, gnomes and brownies for miles around came to buy their cakes. So they made a lot of money, and they decided to give a party.

"We'll ask the toys in the nursery, of course," said Twink. So an invitation was sent to all the toys—to the brown teddy bear, the black golliwog, the green duck, the sailor doll, the golden-haired doll and twelve wooden soldiers. How excited they were!

"I shall wear my best pink ribbon!" said the bear.

"I shall wear a daisy in my button-hole," said the golly.

"We shall polish up our helmets," said the wooden soldiers.

Well, the toys did all they said, and just before it was time to climb out of the window to go to the party they looked at one another to make sure they all were neat and clean.

And then a terrible thing was discovered! The teddy bear had lost one of his brown glass eyes!

"Oh, Teddy, you look awful!" said the golly. "You've lost one of your glass eyes. You can't go to a party with only one eye."

"I thought I felt a bit funny," said the bear, in dismay. "I couldn't see as well as usual. Oh, what am I to do?"

"There's still half an hour before we start," said the sailor doll. "We'll hunt for your eye. I expect we shall soon find it." They began to hunt. They looked in the dolls' house, but it wasn't there. They looked in the toy farm-yard, and asked the toy hens if they had seen it, but it wasn't there. They hunted under the edges of the carpet in case it might have rolled there, but it couldn't be found anywhere.

The poor bear sat down and cried tears out of the eye he had left.

"I can't possibly go to a party with only one eye," he sobbed. "What shall I do? I did so want to go and eat some lovely peppermint cakes."

"Don't cry, Bear dear," said the kind-hearted golden-haired doll, putting her arm round the weeping bear. " We'll get you something else for an eye."

" Oh, will you? " asked the bear, cheering up. " What can I have? "

The toys hunted about. They found a pin with a glass head and brought that to the bear. But he wouldn't have it.

"No," he said, " it's sharp and would prick me. That won't do."

Then a wooden soldier found a silver thimble, but the bear wouldn't have that either.

" I couldn't see out of a thimble eye," he said. " I am sure I couldn't."

Then the golliwog brought a bead, but it was too small. The bear thought it would make him look silly. By that time it was getting near the hour to go to the party and the toys began to feel worried.

Then the sailor doll cried out in glee. The toys crowded round him. He pointed to a little brown shoe belonging to Peggy, the small girl whose nursery they all lived in.

" Let's take this brown button off Peggy's shoe! "
cried the sailor doll. " Peggy wouldn't mind, I'm
sure. The golden-haired doll can easily sew the
button on the bear for an eye, and it would look
lovely."

Well, everyone thought that was a fine idea,
even the bear. So the golden-haired doll cut off
the button from the shoe and then borrowed a
needle and thread from Peggy's little work-box.
She sewed so neatly and so gently that the bear
didn't even feel it, and when she had finished
there he was with a fine new button eye, as hand-
some as ever!

" I can see out of it quite well! " cried the bear,

delighted. "It's as good as my other eye! Hurray! Now I can go to the party!"

"Quite time too," said the golliwog, looking at the nursery clock. "We shall be two minutes late. Never mind, it isn't good manners to be too early."

Off they all went, the teddy bear as proud as could be of his new eye. He looked a bit funny really, with one eye of glass, and the other made of a shoe button, but nobody seemed to notice it, so it didn't matter.

The party was simply lovely. All the cakes were peppermint, but as they were really most delicious no one got tired of them. There was

lemonade to drink, and games to play, and once the golliwog shouted so loudly that he woke up Spot the dog who lay asleep in his kennel nearby, and he began to bark.

The teddy bear had to run and tell him it was all right. Spot growled and lay down again before he had waked up any of the grown-up folk.

At last the party was over. Each guest was given a bag of peppermints to take away, and the toys climbed happily into the nursery again, all smelling very strongly of peppermint. They soon fell asleep and the teddy bear was so tired that he snored very gently.

In the morning Peggy looked for her shoes. " Oh, bother! " she cried. " There's a button gone! "

" Look for it, then," said Nurse. " It was on last night, I'm sure. It can't be far away."

But Peggy couldn't find the button anywhere—until at last she happened to see her teddy bear looking at her with one glass eye—and one brown button eye! She picked him up and looked at him closely.

Yes, he had her shoe-button for an eye! What a very funny thing!

The bear looked at her so pleadingly that Peggy knew he was asking her something.

"All right, Bear dear," she whispered. "I won't take my button! You shall keep it for your eye—but I wish I knew who sewed it on for you, and where you have been, because you *DO* smell of peppermints!"

The bear was so pleased to keep his eye. He put his hand in his pocket, when Peggy wasn't looking, and took out his precious bag of peppermints. He put them on Peggy's chair, and there she found them when she went to sit down!

She looked at the teddy bear—and he winked at her with his brown button eye!

"Oh, thank you, Bear!" she whispered to him. "You may be sure I won't give your secret away!"

And she didn't.

THE OLD SHIPWRECK TREE

In Bluebell Wood there stood an old oak tree
that was very easy to climb. Mollie and John
called it the Shipwreck Tree, because they used
to pretend that when they were up in its branches
they were on a raft out at sea, looking for land.

"We've been shipwrecked, Mollie," John said.
"Our ship has gone down, and we are on a raft,
looking out for an island where we can land safely
and find coco-nuts to eat."

"And perhaps treasure hidden on the island!"
said Mollie. "Ooh, what fun!"

They used to climb up very high and then look out over the country-side, pretending that it was all sea. Then suddenly Mollie would shout:

" Land ahoy! Land ahoy! "

It was a most exciting game, and whenever they could go to Bluebell Wood they always ran to the old Shipwreck Tree and climbed it. The wind swayed them about in the tree, and they felt just as if they were on the sea, being swayed about by the waves.

One afternoon they went to Bluebell Wood together. They ran to the Shipwreck Tree and climbed it to play their favourite game.

" I'll be Captain this time, Mollie," said John. " It's my turn. Now let's talk about our poor ship that went down."

" Oh dear, oh dear," said Mollie, " what a dreadful shipwreck that was! How fortunate that we were able to get off on a raft before the ship sank! "

" But we may die of hunger and thirst before we reach land! " said John, pretending to be very worried. " Did we bring any food, Mollie? "

" Not a crumb! " said Mollie, sighing deeply. " Oh, if only we could see land somewhere! Look again, John! "

John stood up on his branch and looked over the country-side.

Suddenly he shouted in excitement :

" Land ahoy! Land ahoy! "

" Hurrah! " cried Mollie. " We will land and find some coco-nuts to eat, and perhaps some bananas."

"And maybe we'll find some treasure to take back home when we're rescued!" said John.

"Ooh, I wish we could," said Mollie. "It's nice to pretend, John, but I do wish we could *really* find some treasure, don't you?"

"It only happens in books," said John. "Come on, let's go down and pretend to explore the island. Bump! We've landed on the shore, Mollie. Get off the raft."

Mollie was just going to scramble down when John caught hold of her arm. "Sh!" he said in a whisper. "There's somebody coming. Let's pretend they're savages on the island! We'd better stay here till they've gone!"

As quiet as mice the two children sat up in the tree. They heard the sound of someone moving in the wood below. Then a man carrying a sack came into sight. And goodness me, he sat down right under the Shipwreck Tree! How the children hoped he wouldn't look up and see them!

Then they heard more footsteps and soon another man came up to the first one. They began

to talk in very low tones. The children could
hardly hear a word, but they felt sure that the
men were wondering what to do with their sack.

"Well, it's best to hide it here for the night,"
said the first man at last, in a louder voice.
"No one will come to this spot till to-morrow,
anyhow."

"All right. Put it under that thick gorse bush
there," said the second man. They moved off to
a thick bush and pushed the sack underneath it.
They pulled the bush down over it to hide it, and
then they went off together.

The children looked at one another. What an adventure! What was in that sack? They were very glad the men hadn't seen them!

" Is it safe to land and find the treasure, Captain? " whispered Mollie.

" I'll just spy and see if the savages have gone! " said John. He stood up in the tree and looked. " Yes! They are going down the lane beyond the wood. It's all clear! "

Down scrambled the two excited children, and ran to the gorse bush. They pulled out the sack and opened it. And whatever do you think there

was in it! Silver spoons and forks, silver dishes and vases, and silver cigarette-boxes!

"Goodness! Those men must have been burglars!" said John. "We'd better tell the policeman. Come on. We can't carry the sack—it's too heavy. Help me to take it to another bush ; then if the men come back they won't find it where they hid it!"

They hid it under another bush and then ran off to the village. They went to the policeman's house and told him what they had found. He went back with them to Shipwreck Tree and pulled out the sack.

"Yes!" he said. "It's a whole lot of things that have been stolen from people's houses lately! Aha! I'll fill the sack with stones and get another man here to watch for those thieves to come back. What a surprise they'll get!"

He popped the things into another sack he had brought and went home with the children. He told their mother what they had done, and she was very proud of them.

B

"I expect Uncle Dick's silver cigarette-box is among those things," she said. "He had it stolen last week. How pleased he will be to get it back!"

Those two thieves were caught when they went back for the sack. All the things were taken back to their owners, and everyone was told about the two children up in the Shipwreck Tree.

And one day what do you think arrived on the carrier's van? You'll never guess! Why, a real raft, a proper one that would float! With it was a note signed by all the people who had got back

their stolen things, and this is what the note said :
" With love to Mollie and John, hoping they will
find it useful next time they are shipwrecked! "

How excited those two children were! They
took the raft straight out to the big duck-pond, and
floated it. It held them both quite safely, and
away they sailed on the pond, scattering all the
ducks.

I hope they won't *really* be shipwrecked, don't
you?

SKIPPO'S PRANK

SKIPPO was an elf who lived in a tiny shop not far from the royal palace. He sold dancing-spells at sixpence a time. They were very good little spells for those who wanted to dance and didn't know how to.

"All you have to do," Skippo would say, "is to put one of my little spells into your shoe. Then you will find that your legs will do most beautiful dances, and you will not feel ashamed because you don't know how to dance."

Skippo sold a lot of spells, and with the money he bought his food and clothes. He was very fond of fried onions and he cooked these every night for himself.

Now when he left his kitchen door and window open the wind often blew the smell of his frying onions into the window of Princess Goldilocks' nursery, at the back of the Fairy King's palace. She didn't like the smell at all, and her nurse begged the King to ask Skippo to close his door and window when he wanted to cook his onions.

So the King sent for Lord High-and-Mighty, the Chamberlain, and bade him go at once to Skippo's shop and tell him about the onions.

Lord High-and-Mighty was annoyed at having to go. He thought that one of the footmen could have gone. But as he didn't dare to disobey the King, he set off, frowning hard, and stepping out slowly and haughtily.

He was a big Chamberlain, stout and red-faced, and his clothes always looked as if the buttons were bursting off. He walked down the village street in his high boots, looking down his nose at everyone, until he came to Skippo's shop.

He went inside and rapped loudly on the counter. Skippo ran to see what was wanted.

" Skippo," said Lord High-and-Mighty, " please shut your door and window when cooking your disgusting onions each evening. The smell makes the Princess feel faint, and the King is very angry about it."

Now this was untrue, for although the Princess didn't like the smell, it certainly didn't make her feel faint, and the King wasn't at all angry.

Skippo went red.

" My onions aren't disgusting," he said. " They're as good as yours! "

" I don't eat onions," said the Chamberlain. " Nasty, common things! Ugh! Only horrid little elves like you eat such things! "

" Tell that to the King! " said Skippo rudely. " Why, he had onions with his steak the other day. I know, because the cook told me, and she's my sister. So there, Mr. Clever! "

Well, you should have seen the Lord High Chamberlain's face. It really was quite green!

" I shall go at once to report your rudeness to His Majesty! " he said, and he turned to go.

Skippo was frightened. He knew that he had no right to speak like that. Quick as lightning he ran to the door and opened it. He bowed low as the Chamberlain stalked out, and he slipped a little dancing-spell into one of the Chamberlain's high boots as he passed by! Lord High-and-Mighty didn't see him—oh no, he was too quick for that.

Half-way down the street the spell began
to work. You should have seen the Chamberlain! His legs suddenly began to throw
themselves about! They kicked and stamped, they
jigged and jumped, taking him along with them.
He was too surprised to say a single word!

How everyone stared! Then they all began to
laugh, for the Chamberlain was nobody's favourite. They followed him down the street, and
whenever one of his legs kicked very high in the
air they clapped their hands in glee.

Suddenly there came a grand carriage rolling
down the street. It was the King's! He was in
it and so was the Queen. When they saw Lord
High-and-Mighty gambolling and capering in such
a strange way they exclaimed in surprise.

The King stopped the carriage and leaned out.

" What are you doing, Lord High-and-Mighty? "
he asked.

" N-n-n-nothing! It's my legs! " said the poor
Chamberlain, and to his great horror his right leg
jerked itself up high and kicked the King's crown

off! Oh dear me, how everyone trembled to see such a thing! The King couldn't believe his eyes.

"Pick up my crown at once, and stop behaving in such a silly way," he commanded the Chamberlain. But the poor man couldn't pick up the crown, for as soon as he danced near enough to it his foot kicked the crown even further away.

"He's got one of Skippo's dancing-spells in his boot!" suddenly cried a near-by pixie. "That's what's the matter with him. He came out of Skippo's shop. I saw him. Skippo has slipped a spell into his boot!"

The King drove at once to Skippo's shop, and very soon the naughty little elf had confessed.

"How dare you do such a thing!" roared the King. "How dare you, I say! Pack up your spells and leave my kingdom at once. I won't have you here!"

The elf packed up his belongings and then, with the tears running down his face, he swung his sack on to his back and walked down the road to the gates of Fairyland. The Lord High Chamberlain saw him go, and he shook his fist at him, for the dancing-spell was still as strong as ever, and his legs were kicking about all over the place, making him very much out of breath.

"You can stay out of Fairyland until Lord High-and-Mighty forgives you," said the King to Skippo. The elf sighed and wept faster than ever, for he knew that the Chamberlain would never, never forgive him.

He is in our world now with his dancing-spells. They are not strong enough for *our* legs, so who do you think he gives them to? To the little lambs in the spring-time! Have you seen how they jump and frisk about, enjoying themselves immensely?

It's no wonder they do, for Skippo has slipped a dancing-spell into their little hoofs, and they skip in the sunshine as happy as can be.

Look over the hedge and watch them. If you look hard enough, you might even see Skippo, leaning against an old sheep, half asleep in the sunshine!

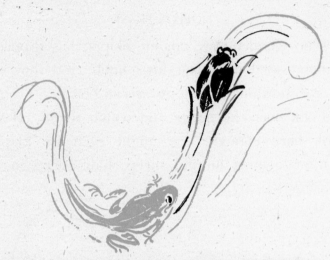

THE TADPOLE AND THE DUCKLING

THERE was once a foolish tadpole who lived in a little pond with a great many frogs, some minnows, hundreds of water-snails, six white ducks and three yellow ducklings.

He was a little nuisance, that tadpole. He would keep putting his blunt little nose into everything. He asked the snails why they wore shells, and he told the minnows that he had overheard the sticklebacks saying they would fight them and stick their sharp little spines into them. He chased a big black water-beetle all over the pond, and made it so frightened that it rose to the surface, spread its wings and flew away!

The tadpole didn't like the croaking noise made by the frogs. In fact, he didn't like the frogs at all, because they took no notice of him, and wouldn't answer any of his questions.

" Those frogs are stuck up," said the cheeky tadpole to a water-snail. " I'm tired of them. They take up a lot of room, they make an ugly croaking noise, and they don't take the slightest notice when I speak to them."

" I don't wonder," said the snail. " I think you're a silly busybody. Go and swim with the other tadpoles and leave the frogs alone. You ought to know better than to interfere with them."

The tadpole butted the snail with his head. He was angry—but the snail simply coiled himself up in his shell and laughed at him.

The tadpole swam off. As he went he saw a strange and frightening sight. One of the big white ducks suddenly put its head under the water.

caught hold of a frog and ate him! Oh my! The
tadpole shook from nose to tail.

Then he swam off to a minnow and told him
what he had seen.

" Didn't you know that ducks ate frogs? " said
the minnow. " You *are* a little silly! "

" Well," thought the tadpole, swimming off,
" I'm glad that ducks eat frogs. Yes, I am! I
shall go and make friends with one of those little
yellow ducklings, and then I will tell her where
she can find frogs to eat. I will soon have the
pond cleared of those stuck-up frogs! Ho ho! "

Silly little tadpole! He thought himself so clever
and yet he didn't even know that tadpoles grew
into frogs! Off he swam to the smallest yellow
duckling, quite determined to do away with every
single frog in the pond.

" If all those silly frogs were gone, the pond-
snails and the fishes might make me their king,"
thought the tadpole. " I am clever and I know a
lot. When I am a very big tadpole I shall be grand
and wise. I would like to be king of the pond."

He swam up to the duckling. She was very
small, but even so she was much larger than the
tadpole. She listened to all he had to say.

"I don't eat frogs yet," said the duckling. "I
am too small. I only eat water-insects, you know.
But later on, in a few weeks' time, when I am big,
I shall be glad of a good meal of frogs. Be friends
with me, dear tadpole, and when I am big I will
be only too glad to do as you say, and eat all the
frogs in the pond. Come and talk to me each
morning."

So the tadpole proudly swam to the duckling
each day and talked to her. He felt so grand
about it that he could hardly say a word to the

minnows or the snails—and they were very glad
to be rid of him. How they smiled to see him
friends with a duckling!

The weeks went by. The duckling grew big.
Her feathers turned from yellow to cream. She was
a pretty little duck. The tadpole altered, too.
He became bigger. He grew back legs and then he
grew front legs. His tail became shorter and
shorter. And at last he was a little frog!

But he didn't know it. He was so proud of
being friends with a duckling that he no longer

talked to his brothers and sisters, the other tad-poles. They would have told him that he was already a little frog. But no, he was too grand altogether!

One day the duckling was very hungry, and she told the tadpole so.

" Ho! " said the tadpole, pleased. " Well, would you like a good meal of frogs today? I know where some are hiding in the weed. I will take you there and you shall feast on them. The sooner they are gone the better, for I want to be king of this pond."

" Take me to the frogs," said the duckling eagerly. So the tadpole took her to the weed.

" Put your head under the water and look in the weed," he cried. " You will see the frogs there, and can feast on them! "

The duckling did as she was told. But as soon as the frogs in the weed saw her yellow feet pad-dling near them they fled away fast. Only the tadpole was left, and he, of course, was no longer really a tadpole, but a little frog.

c   B.S.

The duckling saw him and caught him in her beak, thinking him to be one of the frogs she had come to catch.

" Let me go, let me go! " cried the little tadpole-frog. " It's I, your friend! "

" What, you're the tadpole who spoke to me! " quacked the duck. " I don't believe it! You're a frog like the rest of them. Look at yourself."

The tadpole saw his feet, and found that his long tail had gone. He was indeed a frog. What a dreadful thing! Who could have told him he would turn into a frog? After all his wonderful plans, it was really dreadful! How everyone in the pond must have laughed at him!

" Yes, I am a frog now," he said sadly. " I thought I should be a tadpole all my life. I didn't know I had turned into a frog. I was too clever. Let me go, dear duckling! "

" Not I! " said the duckling. " You said I could eat all the frogs in the pond and I shall begin with *you*! Nobody will miss such a little silly as you, I'm sure! "

With that she tossed up her head and swallowed the foolish frog.   That was the end of him.

All the fishes and the frogs who had seen this shook their heads and looked solemn.

"He deserved it," they said.   "We are not in the least sorry for him."   And neither am I!

THE MEDDLESOME TOYS

PETER came into the nursery with his kite and flung it down on the floor.

"I can't fly this kite properly," he said to Nurse. "It isn't made quite right. Perhaps Daddy can alter it for me so that it will fly nicely."

"Well, put it away in the cupboard and I'll ask him," said Nurse. "I think there is something wrong with it myself. Daddy can easily put it right for you."

Peter threw the kite into the toy cupboard. It was very cross. When the night came it began to grumble.

" There's nothing wrong with me! " it said.
" I'm all right. That boy can't fly me properly,
that's all! "

Now there really *was* something wrong with the
kite. It would fly up a little way and then would
dive down with a bump. It hadn't been made
quite properly. But the kite went on grumbling.

" I'm quite all right. It's that silly boy. If
any of you toys knew how to fly me, I'd soon
show you I was all right," said the kite.

Now the teddy bear had rather a good opinion
of himself. " Well," he said, " I'm sure *I* could
fly you. I've sometimes thought that Peter is
really rather stupid. Fancy not being able to fly
a kite! We toys could, I'm sure! "

" Don't be so conceited," said a lazy little voice
—it was the toy cat who was speaking. " Peter's
as clever as any other boy of seven! You're not
nearly as clever as he is, Teddy, so be quiet."

" Ho! " said the bear angrily. " So I'm conceited, am I? I couldn't fly the kite, you say?
Don't be silly! "

" Yes, don't be silly," said the curly-haired doll, who was very fond of the teddy. " You talk too much, Cat."

" If the bear says he's clever enough to fly the kite, I believe him," said the plush elephant, waving his trunk about.

" So do I," said the big wooden soldier.

" Well, I think the *cat* is right," said the timid bunny. " Anyway, what does it matter? None of us is going to be so silly as to try to fly the kite, surely! "

" Ho, is that what you think? " asked the bear rudely. " Well, think again, Bunny. It's a fine windy night and I'm going to take the kite and fly him, so there! "

" And we'll come with you! " cried the curly-haired doll, the plush elephant and the wooden soldier.

" You're welcome to go! " said the cat, the bunny, the clown and the Dutch doll. " You'll be sorry, that's all, for trying to be so clever! "

The bear said nothing more. He picked up the excited kite and marched out of the nursery

followed by the elephant, the soldier and the doll.
He went into the garden, and made his way to a
little hillock, still followed by his friends.

"Where's the string?" said the bear. "Oh,
here it is. Now we'd better all hold on to it, because if the kite flies high, as it surely will, I shan't
be strong enough to hold it myself."

"Are you ready, Kite?" called the elephant.

"Yes," said the kite. "I'm waiting for the next
puff of wind. Unwind a good bit of string, please."

The wind came. Puff! The kite flew up into
the air, and the wind gave another puff. Higher
still flew the kite, and the teddy bear tried to
unroll the string—but, alas, he got it into a knot,
and couldn't undo it. Puff! went the wind again,
and the kite flew higher still.

The teddy bear was dragged off his feet, and
the elephant, the doll and the soldier were jerked
into the air, too, holding on to the string for all
they were worth! What a shock for them!

Puff! The wind blew again, and the kite
dragged all the toys through the air.

Then it suddenly lost its balance and dived

down to the ground, just as it had kept doing with Peter that morning. Bump! It struck its head on the ground and lay still.

The toys fell to the earth, too—but alas for them, the duckpond was just below them, and they all fell into it—splash!

It wasn't very deep, and they waded out, very muddy and very wet. They didn't say a word to each other. They picked up the kite and walked home.

There was still a little fire in the nursery, and the toys sat down close to it, shivering.

" Whatever have you been doing? " asked the toy cat in astonishment.

" Nothing," said the bear crossly.

" They couldn't fly me after all," said the kite angrily. " Silly creatures! They hung on to the string, and pulled me down! "

" We *didn't* pull you down! " cried the doll. " You dragged us over the pond and then made us fall into it. You're a mean nasty kite! "

" Ha ha! " laughed the cat and the bunny.

"Ho ho!" roared the clown and the Dutch doll. "What a joke! So you all fell into the duck-pond! Well, it serves you right for meddling!"

The other toys said nothing. They were still cold and wet. They dried themselves as best they could, and then crept back to the toy cupboard, quite ashamed of themselves. They knew perfectly well they shouldn't have meddled with the kite.

In the morning Peter and his Daddy came into the nursery and Peter pulled out his kite.

"See, Daddy," he said, "there's something wrong with it."

"Yes," said his Daddy. "This string should be tied *here*, look—and this one *here*! Then the kite will be all right. It could never fly as it was. Nobody could fly it, not even I!"

"Did you hear that?" whispered the toy cat to the bear, giving him a nudge. "Well, Mr. Clever, no wonder you couldn't fly the kite last night! Ho, Mr. Meddlesome, what a silly you are!"

The teddy bear said nothing, but he went red
right to the back of the ears.

"Squeak!" said the bunny in his timid little
voice. "Mr. Bear, you're not so clever as you
thought you were! Ho ho!"

The bear rubbed a tear out of his blue glass
eyes. He didn't like being laughed at.

"GRR-rrr-rrr! he said. "I shan't meddle again,
I promise you!"

And he didn't!

THE MONEY-BOX PIG

THE pig that stood on the nursery mantelpiece wasn't just a pig—he was a money-box, too. In the middle of his back was a slit and pennies and halfpennies slipped in there quite easily. He felt a very light pig when he was empty, and a very heavy pig when he was full.

The toys didn't think much of him, and hardly ever spoke to him, which hurt him very much. And then when the toys planned a fine party one night and didn't ask the money-box pig to go, he was dreadfully offended.

"Why can't I come?" he shouted from the mantelpiece. "I want to come!"

"Only toys are coming," said the golliwog. "You're not a toy."

"Well, what am I, then?" asked the pig crossly. "I'm not a real pig, am I?"

"No," said the golliwog.

"And I'm not an ornament, like a vase of flowers, am I?" asked the pig.

"No," said the golliwog. "I don't know what you are, but you're not a toy, so we don't want you. You're a silly creature, with your pink spots and your curly tail."

The pig nearly burst with rage.

"What about you, with your black face and staring eyes?" he shouted, dancing about on the mantelpiece till all the pennies inside him rattled and clinked.

"Be quiet—you'll wake the children!" said the golliwog angrily. "And don't say such rude things to me. I may have a black face and staring eyes, but Philip and Mollie are very fond of me. They both love me dearly."

"And don't they love me, too?" asked the pig.

"How could they love a creature like you, covered with silly pink spots, and made of cold china?" asked the golliwog scornfully. "Nobody could hug a thing like you!"

The money-box pig thought his heart was broken when he heard the golliwog say that the children didn't love him. Didn't he guard their precious pennies for them? Didn't he stand up all day on the mantelpiece holding their heavy pennies? Well, well, well, it was a sad thing to hear that they didn't love him after all he did for them.

"If they don't love me, I don't want to stay here," he said sadly. "I shall go away to some other nursery where the children will like a money-box pig. Good-bye, toys, I shan't see you again."

The little money-box pig walked along the mantelpiece, climbed down the back of a chair and jumped on to the floor. All the pennies rattled and he nearly fell over.

He walked along the floor to the door. The toys stared after him as he went out.

"You shouldn't have been so unkind to him,"

said the bear to the golliwog. "He isn't a bad little chap really."

"And he's awfully good at looking after the children's pennies," said the big doll.

"I don't know what Philip and Mollie will say when they find that their money-box is gone," said the clockwork clown. "He's got all their money inside him, you know. They are saving up to buy their mother a birthday present, and they will be dreadfully upset to find it's all gone with the money-box pig."

"Ooh my!" said the golliwog in dismay. "Of course he's got the money with him. Goodness, now what are we to do?"

"It was your fault for being so unkind to him," said the white rabbit. "You'd better go and get him back before he falls into a puddle and gets drowned."

"Well, none of you wanted him to come to our party tonight," said the golliwog, "so it's as much your fault as mine. We'd better all go after him."

So off they all went, out of the nursery door. They found the pig crying by himself at the top of the stairs. They were too steep for him to climb down.

"Pig, don't run away," begged the golliwog. "We want you back."

"Think how upset Philip and Mollie will be in the morning to find you and their pennies all gone," said the big doll.

"You s-s-s-said that the ch-ch-children didn't l-l-love me!" wept the little pig.

"Of course they love you and trust you, or they wouldn't give you their pennies to hold," said the clown. "They never give *us* their pennies—only

you. You are very honoured."

The pig cheered up a little.

" Well, I'm glad you think the children do love me a little," he said. " But I think I'll run away, all the same, because I don't like living in a nursery where the toys think I'm not worth asking to parties. Good-bye. Tell the children I'm sorry to take their pennies with me, but I don't know how to get them out of my middle."

He took a few steps towards the stairs. The golliwog pulled him back and put his arm round him.

" Dear money-box pig," he said, " listen to us. We are fond of you really. We don't want to lose you."

"Will you ask me to your party then?" said the pig.

"Yes, you shall come," said the golliwog.

"But I haven't anything pretty to wear," said the pig, beginning to cry again. "I shall feel funny without a party dress."

"The golliwog shall let you wear his red coat," said the doll. "It was he who sent you away, so he ought to do something to make up for it. You shall wear his red coat."

"I should like that," said the pig. He and all the toys walked back to the nursery. The doll made the golly take off his fine red coat, and they put it on the pig. He poked his front legs through the sleeves, and looked very grand indeed.

They had a glorious party. The pig danced so much that all the pennies inside jingled like mad. In fact, he danced so gaily that he didn't hear the cock crow! So he couldn't get back to the mantel-piece in time, and when the cock crew he fell fast asleep in the middle of the nursery floor, still wearing the golliwog's red coat! He did look funny.

Philip and Mollie found him there when they ran into the nursery in the morning—and how astonished they were!

"Look! Pig's got Golly's coat on!" cried Mollie. "And how did he get from the mantelpiece to the floor? What a funny thing! Hallo, little money-box pig! We've come to take out the pennies inside you today, because we're going to buy Mummy's birthday present this morning!"

Well, wasn't the little pig glad that he hadn't run away after all, when he heard that! He knew that the children would have been very unhappy if they hadn't been able to go and buy their present. He beamed at them and nearly danced round the nursery with joy.

"You shall keep your red coat on," said Philip, putting him back on the mantelpiece. "You look fine in it!"

Poor Golly! He hasn't got his coat back yet! But he shouldn't have been so mean to the little money-box pig, should he?

WHAT HAPPENED TO A SMILE

BENNY was a thin little boy, and he had never
had an overcoat in his life. He had only once had
a penny to spend, and he had never forgotten that
day. He was quite happy, though, and what his
mother would do without him she really didn't
know.

"You know, Mother," said Benny, "I really
don't mind being poor except for one thing—and
that is I can never give anybody anything! I
can't give Lucy next door a Christmas present at
Christmas-time, and I can't give Tom a birthday

present. I can't even give the old blind man at the corner a halfpenny, and I wish I could."

" Why, Benny! " said his mother, in surprise, " What does it matter if you can't give people presents and money? You can give them other things, can't you? "

" What things? " asked Benny.

" Well, you can give them a bright smile, for instance," said his mother. " You can give them a hand with their parcels. You can give a polite ' Good morning ' to the people in the road. Look at that poor, ugly old Mister Grim who lives in the next street—nobody ever smiles at him, and I'm sure he must be sad and lonely, without a friend in the world! "

Benny thought about what his mother said. Yes, it was quite true. Although he hadn't any money at all to buy things for other people, he could give smiles and kindness. He made up his mind to begin that very day.

He went out shopping for his mother that morning. He took her net bag with him, because she wanted some potatoes. As he went he kept a look-out for old Mister Grim. Benny was really a bit frightened of him, because he had such thick, shaggy eyebrows, and he frowned so crossly.

Sure enough, down the street came Mister Grim, frowning hard, as usual. And just as he reached Benny the little boy raised his cap, said " Good morning," most politely, and smiled. Benny had a fine smile. It made you feel happy and good when he smiled at you.

Mister Grim was so surprised that he forgot to smile back. He just stared at Benny as if he

couldn't believe his eyes. The little boy went on his way, glad that he had smiled, but disappointed that Mister Grim hadn't smiled back.

" It was a waste of a smile! " said Benny to himself. But it wasn't. A smile is never wasted —never. Hear what happened to this one, and you'll see.

Mister Grim went on his way. He kept thinking of Benny's smile, and it warmed his cold, lonely heart. When he got home he went and looked at himself in the mirror. He saw a dirty, untidy, cross old man there. Dear, dear, what a dreadful sight he looked!

" There must be something nice about me, or that little boy wouldn't have given me such a fine smile," said Mister Grim to himself. " Well, I've always thought I was an ugly, cross, sour, bad-tempered old fellow who hated children and hadn't a friend in the world. I wonder—could I possibly be mistaken? "

He looked at himself again, and then a thought came into his head.

" I don't believe I'm as bad as all that! " he
said. " I believe if I was clean and tidy, and
had a nice new suit and my hair cut, I'd be a fine
fellow. That little chap wouldn't have smiled at
me if I had been as bad as everyone makes out."

Well, you should have seen Mister Grim that
day! He took off all his things and had a hot
bath. Then he put on his clothes again, and
shook his head. " I can't tidy these up," he said.
" I will go and get a new suit."

So off he went. He popped into the hair-
dresser's first of all and had his hair cut nicely.
Then he went to Mister Hem, the tailor.

"I want a nice new suit," he said. "Something cheerful and bright. And I want a new hat. Oh, and a new overcoat, too. Please fit me for all these things."

Mister Hem was delighted. Things had been going very badly with him lately, and he hadn't enough work to do. He began to measure Mister Grim and he talked to him happily. So few people ever talked to Mister Grim that he felt more pleased than ever. How fine it was to get a new suit and be measured by a nice friendly tailor like this!

"I think I'll have *two* suits!" he said suddenly.

" Yes, I could really do with two. I'll have one in blue and one in a nice warm brown. And I'll have two hats as well."

Well, Mister Hem couldn't believe his ears! What a lot of money he would make that week! Oh my, it was good news! He would be able to send his little nephew a fine birthday present now. That was good.

Mister Grim left the shop at last, beaming all over his face. Mister Hem, the tailor, sat down and set to work to cut the cloth to make the new suits.

He smiled to himself. " What shall I send Jack for his birthday? Shall I send him a train? No, he's got one. Shall I send him a book? No, I might send him one he's got already. Dear me—what shall I send him, now? "

He cut out the sleeves of a coat and thought hard. " I know! " he said at last. " I will send him money. Yes, I will send him five shillings. Or shall it be seven shillings and sixpence? He is a good boy, and I am fond of him. I shall make much money from these coats. I will send him seven shillings and sixpence!"

Well, when he had done a good deal more work he stopped for his dinner. Then he went out to the post office and he bought some paper money worth seven shillings and sixpence. It was a postal order. Mister Hem put it into an envelope and addressed it to Jack, his little nephew.

What a lot that smile had done already! It had made Mister Grim buy lots of new clothes and feel much happier. It had caused the tailor to feel most delighted, and had made him buy a postal order for seven shillings and sixpence.

Jack didn't expect such a wonderful birthday present from his uncle, the tailor. He didn't expect anything at all, because he knew that Uncle Hem was feeling rather poor. As a matter of fact Jack had almost forgotten he was going to have a birthday, because he was so very unhappy about something.

That something was his puppy dog, Spot. You see, Spot was just over six months old, and so he should have had a licence. Every dog over that age has to have a licence bought for him at the post office for seven shillings and sixpence. And poor Jack hadn't any money at all, and his father couldn't possibly pay for the licence! So he was dreadfully worried, because he loved Spot with all his heart.

"Oh, Spot, if I can't buy you a licence the policeman will come and take you away from me!" he said, hugging the little dog. "All dogs must have licences, and you haven't got one. Oh, why did you grow big so quickly? I can't do without you!"

Spot licked his little master sorrowfully. He didn't know what was the matter, but it nearly broke his heart to see Jack cry.

And now you can imagine what Jack felt like on the next day when his uncle's letter arrived with a postal order for seven shillings and sixpence! What a lot of money! Why—that was the price of a dog licence ; it was, it was!

Inside the envelope with the money was a little note that said :

" Dear Jack,

I don't know what you want for your birthday, so here is some money. Spend it on anything you like, and be happy.

Your loving Uncle,
HEM."

Jack flew round the kitchen in joy, waving the money about, and shouting excitedly to his father and to Spot, who was quite glad to see his little master so happy again. Out they went together to buy the licence, both of them running and jumping for all they were worth!

Jack bought the licence at the post office, and then went down by the river to go to his uncle's shop to thank him for his lovely present.

Now it so happened that Benny was running by the river, too. He was going shopping for his mother again, just as he had done the day before, and the path by the river was a short cut to the shops.

As he ran his foot caught against a piece of tree-trunk, and over he went. He rolled down the river-bank into the river! Splash! In he

went, and the water closed right over his head. He came to the top and shouted for help.

Jack ran down to the water—but someone else was quicker! And that was Spot, the big puppy dog! He had seen Benny fall and had heard the splash. He loved his master so much that he wanted to help all other little boys, and he was going to get Benny out of the river if he possibly could!

Splash! In he went too, and swam to Benny. He caught hold of the boy's coat in his strong teeth and swam steadily back to the bank with him, his four legs striking out gallantly. How everyone cheered! Heaps of people had run down to the river when they had seen Benny fall in, and how glad they were when Spot got him safely to the bank. Jack dragged him up on the grass and Spot licked him all over.

"Good dog, Spot, good dog!" said Jack, very proud of his puppy. "Oh, you deserve your seven-and-sixpenny licence—yes, you do!"

"He's the best dog in the world!" said Benny, hugging him. "He saved me from being drowned! Look how wet I am!"

"Come with me to my uncle's," said Jack. "He lives nearby, and he'll dry you. He's awfully kind."

So Benny went with Jack to his Uncle Hem's, the tailor, and very soon he was standing in front of a big fire, wrapped in a shawl, whilst Mister Hem dried his clothes on a rack in the kitchen.

Whilst they were all talking nineteen to the dozen, who should come in but Mister Grim, to see how his new suits were getting on! He was *so* surprised to see Benny standing by the fire with a towel round his shoulders.

E   B.S.

"Well, well," he said, "if it isn't the nice little boy who smiled at me yesterday! Well, well! What do you think your fine smile did for me, my boy? It made me feel so good that I came in here and ordered a whole lot of new clothes! Didn't I, Mister Hem?"

"You certainly did," said the tailor. "And your order made me very happy, because I knew then I could afford to send my little nephew here some money for his birthday. Did you get the postal order, Jack?"

"Oh, Uncle, yes, I did," cried Jack, hugging the delighted tailor. "I forgot to thank you for it because of all the excitement about Benny falling into the river."

"What are you going to spend it on?" asked his uncle.

"I've spent it already!" said Jack. "I've bought a dog licence for dear old Spot! We were just coming back from the post office when Benny fell into the river. And then Spot jumped in and saved him."

Suddenly everyone was quiet. They were thinking. Most of all Benny was thinking. Presently he spoke.

" My own smile saved me! " he said. " If I hadn't smiled at Mister Grim yesterday, he wouldn't have felt pleased and gone to buy his new clothes. If he hadn't gone to buy them, Mister Hem wouldn't have had the money to send to Jack. And if Jack hadn't had the money, he wouldn't have gone to buy a licence for Spot. And if he hadn't gone to buy the licence for Spot, he wouldn't have been by the river when I fell in and Spot wouldn't have been able to save me from drowning! It was all because of my smile—

the smile my mother told me I ought to give to people, because I had nothing else to give but that! "

" What a wonderful thing! " said Mister Grim. " Who would have thought a smile could do all that? "

" And I thought it was wasted! " said Benny. " But it wasn't. Mother says smiles and kind words are never wasted, and she's right."

Well, what do you think of that? But that wasn't all the smile did, by a long way! Because of that smile Jack, Benny and Spot became the greatest of friends. Mister Hem, the tailor, made such fine coats for Mister Grim that he became famous and had to take a larger shop— and as for Mister Grim himself, he was a different man! He became kind, generous and friendly, and all the children loved to meet him, for he never frowned as he used to do.

And all because of a smile!

SLY THE CAT AND SMART THE DOG

THERE were once two animals who lived in the same house together. One was Sly the Cat, as cunning as her name—and the other was Smart the Dog, but he was *not* quite so clever as his name. Sly was always tricking him in some way, so she always got the best of everything.

One day they went out for a walk together. They were both very hungry, for they had had nothing to eat that morning. They sniffed the air and wondered what they might get to eat.

"What about going to the butcher's to see if there are any bones about?" asked Smart.

" No," said Sly. " You stole some sausages last time, so the butcher won't let us go anywhere near his shop."

They trotted on together—and suddenly Sly lifted her nose in the air and sniffed hard.

" I smell something! " she said. " Sniff, Smart, and see if you smell something, too."

Smart sniffed. Yes, he smelt something. It was very strong.

" It's fish," he said. " Somewhere over by the stream, Sly. Let's go and look."

Off they went, and soon came to where a dozen fish lay on the bank. Sly and Smart were delighted. Smart was going to gobble them up at once, but Sly spoke sharply.

" Be careful, Smart. They may be bad fish and might poison us. Don't eat in a hurry."

Now Sly knew quite well that if the dog began to eat the fish he would gobble them all up before she had even licked the tail of one! So she tried hard to think of a plan to stop him.

" So you really think they are bad fish? "

asked Smart, sniffing. "They do smell rather strong."

"If we ate bad fish, we should have a pain and be dreadfully ill," said Sly solemnly. "What can we do?"

They sat and looked at one another. Sly felt sure the fish were quite all right, and she was anxious not to let the dog begin on them.

"I'll just take a little nibble at one end and see if it's all right," said the dog, at last.

"No, don't! I couldn't bear to see you ill!"

said the cat quickly. "Let *me* have a nibble. I'll
soon know if they are good or not!"

She ran to the fish and began to nibble at one.
Then she sat back and pretended to taste what
she had in her mouth. She suddenly made a face
and began to rock to and fro and cry out :

"Oh, oh, fetch the doctor—the fish is bad!
It's given me a dreadful pain! Oh, I'm poisoned,
I'm poisoned! Oh, fetch the doctor, quick!"

Smart was frightened. He ran to the cat to
comfort her, but she waved him away and rocked
herself to and fro again.

"Fetch the doctor, quick, fetch the doctor!"
she wailed.

Smart ran off in a great hurry. The doctor

lived quite three miles away, so he had a long way to go. He went as fast as he could, puffing and panting, his red tongue hanging out of the corner of his mouth.

"What a good thing we didn't gobble up *all* the fish!" he said to himself. "My, we *should* have been ill!"

As soon as the dog was out of sight Sly began to laugh. She jumped up and went to the fish, and in a few moments she was having the best meal she had had for weeks. How she ate!

She ate a whole fish, and then she ate another. Then she started on a third—and she was just in the middle of it when a loud voice startled her, and she felt a heavy hand on her neck.

"How dare you steal my fish!" cried a cross voice. Sly twisted her head to see who had caught her, and saw that it was a fisherman! He had caught the fish that morning and had left them on the bank whilst he went to untangle his fishing-hook from a tree a little way off.

Poor Sly! The fisherman shook her this way and shook her that. He smacked her hard and he pulled her tail. She mewed loudly, but Smart the Dog was too far away to hear her. No, it was a proper punishment for her!

The fisherman at last put her down on the ground again. Sly was so giddy that she sat where she was put, not daring to move. The fisherman gathered up the rest of the fish, put them into his basket, and went off.

Sly began to weep hot tears, for she felt so bad after her beating. And what would Smart say when he came back and found all the fish gone?

Just as she was sitting there, feeling very sorry for herself, Smart came panting back with the doctor.

"Here's the patient!" he cried to the doctor.
"She nibbled a bit of bad fish, and feels ill."
Then he looked for the rest of the fish to show
the doctor. But it was gone!

Smart looked at Sly. She seemed very fat and
round. Had she got rid of him by a trick, and
eaten all the fish whilst he was gone?

"Where's the fish?" he barked angrily.

"A fisherman came and took it all," said Sly.
"He said he had just caught it this morning."

"Then it couldn't have been bad fish!" said
Smart, in a rage. "It was good fish and you

played a trick on me! I don't believe that a fisherman came at all. I believe you ate all the fish yourself! "

With that he pounced on Sly and bit her tail so hard that she squeaked and fled. After her went Smart, yelping and barking for all he was worth. The doctor stood and stared after them, very angry to think he had come all that way for nothing.

" I shall send them in a great big bill for being so silly," he said, as he tramped home again.

As for Smart and Sly, they soon made up their quarrel and were friends again—but you may be sure that Smart made *Sly* pay the doctor's bill!

THE TWO COCKS

ONCE upon a time there were two cocks in a farmyard. They were fine fellows, called Doodle and Doo. Their red combs stood up from their heads, and their tail-feathers sprouted grandly, shining now blue and now green.

Their voices were very loud. They cried: "Cock-a-doodle-do!" at the very first peep of dawn, and woke up all the farm folk at once. They strutted over the yard, their heads held up and their combs glowing red. Sometimes they fought one another and then the feathers flew in all directions.

They lived with twenty-two red hens. The hens had no fine tail-feathers, but they were pretty, for all that. How they scratched and scraped in the earth, looking for a tiny grain to gobble up! How they ran when they heard Mistress Susan rattling the pail in which she brought their food twice a day!

The two cocks were so alike that you really couldn't tell one from the other—except in their manners. Ah, you could tell which was Doodle and which was Doo then! They might look the same from beak to tail, but their manners were quite different.

Doodle was a greedy cock who didn't care two grains of corn for any of his hens. He scraped in the earth just as they did and if he found a nice big piece of corn, what did he do? Did he call his hens to share it? No, not he! He gave a greedy squawk and gobbled it up himself.

And when Mistress Susan flung handfuls of corn to the fowls, did Doodle see that all the hens got their full share before he ate any? No—the

greedy, ill-mannered bird pushed aside the hungry
hens and gobbled up all he could, even going
so far as to snatch a specially big grain of corn
out of a hen's beak! He was not a nice bird at
all.

But Doo was quite different. If he scraped up
a grain of maize he called to his hens at once and
they all came running. Then he would drop the
maize in front of a hen and she would gobble it
up gratefully. When Mistress Susan threw the
food into the yard Doo never picked up the tiniest
piece himself until he was quite sure every single

one of his hens had had enough. Then he would hurriedly have his meal.

Now one day the farmer said that he wanted a bird for his dinner.

" Master's coming to sup with us tonight," he told his wife. " So we'll have one of those two cocks for dinner, Mistress."

" Very well, George," said Mistress Susan. " Which one will you have? "

" It doesn't matter," said the farmer. " They are as like as two peas."

" Oh, no, Father, they're not! " cried his little girl. " Doodle is a horrid bird. He is greedy and spiteful, and has no manners at all. But Doo is gentle and kind. He always lets the hens eat first."

" Then we'll have Doodle for supper," said the farmer. " Do you know which is which, wife? "

" No, I don't," said Mistress Susan. " But I'll take our Annie with me and she'll tell me."

So Annie went with her mother to the yard.

The two cocks were standing in the sun, enjoying the warmth. They looked exactly alike.

"Well, well," said Mistress Susan. "There's no telling which is which, Annie dear."

"Watch," said Annie, and she threw a handful of corn into the yard. Oh, what a scramble there was! How the hens squawked and clucked! And dear me, what a disgrace the cock Doodle was! He gobbled up all the grains he could see and pecked at the hen next to him, pulling away a tuft of feathers from her neck.

But Doo helped the hens to find the grain. He

gave two pieces to the smallest hen of all, who wasn't very good at pushing and pecking. He really was a perfect gentleman.

"There, Mother!" said Annie, pointing. "See what a difference there is in the cocks! Don't eat Doo, he's so good and kind. Eat Doodle, the greedy ill-natured bird!"

So Doodle was made into a pie for supper, and Doo was left with the hens. Nobody missed Doodle or wanted him back. As for Doo he is still alive, and looking after his hens as well as ever.

And now mother hens say to greedy, ill-mannered chicks : "Be careful! Bad manners are made into a pie, but good ones live for ever!"

MR. MIGGLE'S SPECTACLES

ONCE upon a time there was a gnome called
Mister Miggle. He thought a lot of himself, and
he hoped other people did too—but they didn't!
They thought Mister Miggle was a fat, greedy,
mean old gnome, who always pretended he was
too poor to help anyone.

Mister Miggle was vain. He quite thought
everyone liked him and admired him, but he did
wish they would say so. Nobody ever told him
he was good-looking, and nobody said he was
kind or good.

" I suppose they are too shy to say so to me," he thought, as he walked proudly down the village street, dressed in a new yellow suit, tied up with red ribbons all down the front. " How I wish I knew what everyone was thinking about me! It would be lovely to know. I expect they are thinking how fine I look, and what a grand gnome I am! "

Now it so happened that on that day a pedlar came to Mister Miggle's village, selling all kinds of queer things. He called at Mister Miggle's house after tea, and Mister Miggle looked at his things.

" Here's a broom that will sweep by itself," said the pedlar, showing Miggle a little yellow broom. " Or here's a jug which is always full of new milk."

" No, thanks," said Mister Miggle. " I don't want those."

" Well, what about a pair of spectacles that will tell you what everyone is thinking about you? " said the pedlar, picking up a little red case and opening it. In it lay a pair of big round

spectacles with very peculiar glass that twinkled and blinked all the time.

"Ooh!" said Mister Miggle. "Just what I want! How much?"

"Three pieces of gold!" said the pedlar. "They are very rare, you know."

Mister Miggle put the spectacles on and looked hard at the pedlar. The man immediately thought of something nice about Miggle, for he knew the gnome was reading his thoughts.

Mister Miggle saw what he thought—the pedlar
was thinking: " What a nice gnome! I'm sure
he will be sensible enough to buy my wonderful
spectacles, for they are very cheap indeed! "

Mister Miggle wasn't clever enough to know
that the pedlar was thinking these things on pur-
pose, and he was very pleased. He paid the gold
without a word and the pedlar went off, chuckling to himself, thinking of the dreadful shocks
that Miggle would have when he put the spectacles on and found out what people *REALLY*
thought of him!

Miggle was most excited. He could hardly
sleep that night for thinking of the lovely time he
would have the next day, finding out what everyone thought of him.

" I shall put on my new suit again," he said
to himself. " I look nice in that. Then I will
walk down the street with my spectacles on and see
what everyone is thinking about me."

So the next morning he put on his fine yellow
suit, popped his pointed hat on, and settled his

new spectacles on his nose. Then out he went
down the street.

The first person he met was old Dame Wimple.
Miggle smiled at her and she nodded back. She
didn't say a word. Miggle looked at her through
his glasses to see what she was thinking—and my,
what a shock he got!

" Silly, fat old gnome! " the old dame was
thinking. " I suppose he thinks he looks fine in
that awful suit. What a sight he looks! "

Miggle nearly cried out in horror. Could old

Dame Wimple really be thinking that? No, no, the glasses must be making some mistake!

Round the corner he met Skip and Jump, the little boy pixies who lived at Hallo Cottage. He smiled at them, and they said good morning to him most politely. Mister Miggle looked through his glasses to see what they were really thinking, and again he got a most terrible shock.

" Nasty, mean old thing! " Skip was thinking. " He never gives a little pixie even a ha'penny! "

" What an ugly face old Miggle's got! " Jump was thinking. " I should hate to meet him at night in a dark corner! "

Well ! Miggle was so surprised that he stood quite still and stared at the two little pixies. They were frightened and ran away. Miggle heaved a great sigh and went on.

" I suppose children always think silly things like that," he said to himself. " It's no use taking any notice of them. It's the grown-ups that matter."

At the roadside stood a brownie, selling red apples. Mister Miggle looked at him through his

glasses, hoping to see some really nice thoughts
in his head. But, no, again he was disappointed.

"It's no use asking this mean-looking old
gnome to buy my nice apples," the brownie was
thinking. "He looks a real miser, although he
is so fat."

Mister Miggle was shocked. Did he really look
like a miser? He looked into a mirror set in a shop
window. Yes, his mouth did look rather thin and
mean. Oh, dear, he wasn't having a very nice
morning!

Ah, here came Mister Snoop, his friend. *Now*
he would read some nice thoughts, surely. He

shook hands with Snoop and looked at him through his glasses. Oh goodness! Mister Snoop was thinking no better thoughts than the others.

"So he's got a new suit again," Snoop was thinking. "Why does he always have his suits so tight they look as if they were bursting? And why does Miggle eat so much? He really is much too fat. I'm sure I don't know why I'm friends with him. He's a mean, greedy fellow and I don't really like him at all."

Snoop was very much surprised to see Miggle burst into tears and hurry down the street without a word. He had no idea that the fat little gnome

could see what he was thinking and had been
very much upset by it.

"Well, well," thought Snoop, "what next? He
really is a silly chap, that Miggle."

Miggle dried his eyes under his glasses and
walked up the hill towards Mrs. Lemon's cottage. Mrs. Lemon was out in her garden water-
ing her flowers. Miggle hardly dared to look at
her in case he read something horrid about
himself.

"But she's the kindest person in the village,"
he thought. "So she's sure to be thinking something nice about me. I'll see if she is."

He said good morning to Mrs. Lemon and read
her thoughts. Poor Miggle! He had no luck
that morning for Mrs. Lemon, kindhearted as she
was, was not thinking very nice things about the
foolish, fat gnome.

"Here comes old greedy Miggle," she was
thinking. "Poor old fellow! I wonder if he
guesses how everyone laughs at him and dislikes
him. I believe he thinks we all like him. If only

he knew what we think, he would get a dreadful shock! "

Miggle *did* get a dreadful shock! He looked at Mrs. Lemon as if he couldn't believe his ears and eyes. She was astonished.

" What's the matter? " she asked. " Are you ill? Come into my garden and sit down for a bit."

Mister Miggle read what she was thinking.

" Miggle looks ill," she was thinking. " I suppose as usual he's been eating too much. What a dreadful fellow he is, to be sure! "

Miggle stopped at the gate and spoke sadly to Mrs. Lemon.

" I can see what you are thinking, Lucy Lemon," he said. " I have magic spectacles on. You have been thinking I am a greedy fellow, whom nobody likes. Ah, well, perhaps you are right."

Mrs. Lemon was astonished. She looked at Miggle's spectacles and saw that they were magic ones. She was sorry for the unhappy gnome, for she knew what a lot of shocks he must have had that morning.

"Come in for a minute," she said kindly. "I didn't mean you to see my thoughts—but people can't very well help their thoughts, can they?"

Miggle came in and sat down on a bench. He took off his glasses and looked at Mrs. Lemon.

"Am I a very horrid fellow? he asked.

"You are rather," said Mrs. Lemon, "but you needn't be. If only you wouldn't think so much of yourself, Miggle, and would think a little more of other people, you'd be all right. And you shouldn't eat so much, you know—you're getting

fat and ugly.   You used to be such a good-looking
gnome! "

Miggle was very sad.

" Do you think I could ever be nice? " he asked.

" It's never too late to mend," said Mrs. Lemon.
" You mustn't blame other people for what they
think of you, you know.   It is you that have made
their thoughts about you.   The people in this
village are kindly folk, and it's your own fault if
they think unkindly about you.   What about
trying to turn over a new leaf, Miggle?   Try for
a month and then put on the magic glasses again! "

Miggle said he would try.   He put his glasses
into their case, thanked Mrs. Lemon for helping
him and went sadly home.   He sat down by his
fire and made all sorts of plans.

He wouldn't be so greedy.   He would take
good long walks each day to make himself thinner.
He would be kind and generous to the children
and to the poor people.   He would ask Snoop,
his friend, to help him.

Poor Mister Miggle!   He tried hard for a month

and it wasn't easy. Snoop and Mrs. Miggle helped him, and at last he really felt a bit different. He looked for his magic glasses to put on to see if people were thinking kinder thoughts about him— and they weren't there!

He had lost them—so he never knew what other people were thinking about him after all—but as he really is different, I expect their thoughts are different, too. Don't you?

Nobody knows where those glasses went to. If you should ever come across them, what sort of thoughts would you read in other people's minds if you put those spectacles on? I wonder!

THE VERY CROSS FARMER

SHEILA and David were staying with their Aunt
Susan, down in the country. It was lovely there,
much nicer than living in the town. There were
hundreds of flowers to pick, blackberries getting
ripe, animals to see and exciting things to do.
Sheila and David were very happy.

Everybody was kind to them—except Farmer
Brown, who lived on the farm nearby. Sheila
and David were afraid of him because he was so
cross. One morning they had been walking by
the farm and he had come rushing out at them,
shouting loudly :

" You naughty children! You tiresome children! You've left my field-gate open, and the
cows are out in the corn! "

" We haven't left *any* gate open! " said David.
" We haven't been in any field today, and we
always shut the gates after us."

The farmer shook his fist at them, but didn't
wait to hear what they had to say, for he had to
get his cows out of the corn. Sheila and David
hurried away fast, for they didn't want to be
shouted at again.

Another time, after they had been blackberrying in a field, they met Farmer Brown
again.

" Are you the two children who have been after
my apples? " he asked crossly. " Someone's been
after them again."

" Of course we haven't! " cried Sheila. " We
don't steal! We've been blackberrying, and Auntie
says anyone may pick blackberries."

" Well, you look very like the two children I
saw in my orchard yesterday evening," said the

farmer. "I'm going to spank the next children I see there, so you be careful."

Sheila began to cry and David hurried her away.

"Don't cry," he said, putting his arm round his little sister. "He won't hurt you while I'm here. Besides, we haven't done a single naughty thing since we've been staying with Auntie Susan. He's just mistaken us for two other children, that's all."

"I don't like people to t-talk to me crossly," wept Sheila. "I'm afraid of that nasty, horrid farmer. He's a dreadful, cross man."

David told his Auntie Susan about Farmer Brown, and she told them not to worry about him.

" It's no wonder he doesn't like children," she said. " They're always doing something to annoy him. They bring their dogs down the farm lane in the spring-time, and I couldn't tell you how many little lambs have been scared or bitten by the dogs, to say nothing of the hens and chicks. Then they leave the gates open and let the cows and horses out. Or they steal his fruit. So you see, he thinks all children are a nuisance, because none of them has ever done him a good turn!"

" Well, he's a nasty cross man," said Sheila, wiping her eyes. " I don't like him a bit, and I'll never help him even if I can, so there! "

" Oh, you mustn't talk like that, Sheila," said Auntie, shocked. " You should always help people when you can, even if they are horrid to you."

" Well, I don't expect we shall ever be able to help Farmer Brown," said David, " so there's no need to worry, Sheila! "

But that's where David was wrong. The very next day something happened, and he had to choose whether he would help Farmer Brown or not.

The two children were walking down the lane that ran beside the field where the brown and white cows were grazing, when they heard a dog barking. They looked into the field and saw a big cow lowering her horns at the excited dog. The dog rushed at her and the cow stepped backwards— but she didn't know how near the ditch she was, and she slipped right into the muddy ditch up to her waist.

The dog ran away, and crept through the hedge when he saw the children looking over the gate. He knew quite well that he shouldn't be there. The cow tried to get out of the ditch, but she couldn't. She mooed in fright and tried again.

" Perhaps she has broken her leg," said David anxiously. " Or if she hasn't she might easily break it, if she isn't careful. The ditch is so steep just there."

" What shall we do? " asked Sheila.

" Well—don't you think we ought to go and tell Farmer Brown? " said David. " It's his cow, and cows are valuable."

"That nasty cross man!" cried Sheila, her face going red. "I don't want to help him. I don't care if his old cow dies!"

"Oh, Sheila, you do say dreadful things," said David. "Think of the poor old cow. Even if you don't want to be kind to the farmer, you might be kind to the cow. If you had a broken leg in a ditch you'd want people to be kind to you, wouldn't you?"

"Yes, I should," said Sheila. "Poor cow! Well, I'll be kind to the cow, and you can be kind to the farmer, David. I'll stay and look after the cow, and you can go to the farm."

So David ran off to the farm and left Sheila

standing near the frightened cow. She talked to
it kindly, and it seemed to understand.

"Don't be afraid," she said. "David has gone
to get help for you. You'll soon be all right. Stay
there quietly till someone comes."

David walked into the farm-yard. He was
afraid of the farmer, and his heart beat loudly.
He couldn't see Farmer Brown anywhere, so he
went to the farm-house door and knocked. Goodness me, the farmer himself opened it, and he
frowned when he saw David.

"If you've come to ask for windfall apples you

can go right away again! " he said angrily, and
he slammed the door.

David went very red. This was dreadful. Did
he dare to knock again? Well, if anyone was going
to help that poor old cow, he'd just *have* to knock
again. So he knocked.

The door flew open and out came the farmer
with a stick in his hand—but David stood his
ground and said, very loudly :

" I've just come to say that one of your cows
has fallen into the ditch, and would you please
come and help her out? "

The farmer stared at David in surprise.

" In the ditch! Wait a moment! I'll get Joe
to come and help and we'll pull her out."

He called " Joe! Joe! " loudly, and presently a
man came running into the yard. " Bring a
rope and come to the Long Field," said the farmer.
" One of the cows is in the ditch."

David took him to the place where the cow lay.
Sheila was still there. She ran away when she
saw the farmer coming.

" Who's that little girl? " said the farmer to David.

" That's my sister, Sheila," said David. " She said she would stay and keep the cow company whilst I went to fetch you. She's run away because she's afraid of you."

" Hmph ! " said the farmer, and he took the rope from Joe. He twisted it cleverly round the cow's horns, and told Joe to get into the ditch and push the cow when he pulled.

" Hup there! Hup there! " shouted Farmer Brown suddenly to the cow, and he pulled the rope wound round her horns. Joe pushed hard at the same time and the cow came out of the ditch with a run. Farmer Brown sat down suddenly and David began to laugh, for it really was a funny sight to see.

The farmer wasn't a bit cross, for a wonder. He roared with laughter, and so did Joe. The cow walked away to join the others.

" She's all right," said Farmer Brown. " But if she'd struggled much longer she would have

cracked a leg, for sure. Well, now, boy, it's good
of you to have come and got help for my cow.
Thank you very much. Come back and have some
tea with my old woman and me. She's baked hot
gingerbread today. You and your little sister will
like it."

David was so surprised to hear Farmer Brown
speak so kindly. He beckoned to Sheila and she
came up, still half afraid.

" Farmer Brown wants us to go and have tea at
the farm-house," he said. " Shall we go and ask
Auntie if we may? There's hot gingerbread, he
says."

" Of course, we'll go and ask Auntie, this very

minute!" shouted the farmer, laughing. "Don't
you be afraid of me, little girl. My bark's worse
than my bite!"

And to Sheila's astonishment he suddenly picked
her up and sat her on his shoulder! Then he
galloped off up the lane like one of his great big
cart-horses! Sheila loved it, and cried out in
delight. It was so exciting.

Auntie Susan said of course they could go to the
farm for tea, so off they went. And after a perfectly
glorious tea of bread and jam and cream, hot
gingerbread and buttered buns, Farmer Brown
took them off to milk the cows with him.

"I thought you were so horrid," said Sheila,
when she went with him to milk the cows, "but
you're a very nice farmer, after all. I'm glad
we helped you when your cow fell into the
ditch."

"I'm cross when children are naughty, but I'm
fond of them when they're good and helpful,"
said Farmer Brown. "You shall just see what a
fine time I'll give you now!"

And he certainly did! David and Sheila rode
his horses, milked the cows, fed the hens, picked the
apples and ate them, too! They *were* glad they
had helped the farmer that day!

THE SQUIRREL AND THE MOUSE

FRISKY, the squirrel, was busy in the nut trees. There were a great many nuts that year, and Frisky was enjoying them very much. He was gnawing through the shells with his sharp teeth, eating the juicy kernels inside and then throwing away the empty shells.

When he had eaten all he wanted, he turned his bright black eyes up to the sky. It was grey and wintry-looking, although it was only October.

" I think," said Frisky, " I will pick some nuts
and store them away for winter. Then when I
wake up from my long winter nap, on some sunny
January day, I shall be able to find the nuts I've
hidden, and have a fine feast. Yes, that's a good
idea."

He began to pick some ripe hazel-nuts—but he
hadn't picked more than two or three when a
little voice called up to him :

" Frisky! I say, Frisky, can you spare me a
few nuts? I'm so hungry! "

The squirrel looked down from his tree. He saw
Brownie, the wood-mouse, sitting up on his hind-
legs, calling to him.

But Frisky was selfish. There were heaps of
nuts, far more than he could eat or hide, but he
didn't want to give any to Brownie. So he shook
his head.

" I'm sorry, Brownie," he said. " There are
only enough for me."

" Don't be mean and selfish," said the wood-
mouse. " Throw a few down, Frisky. I'd love

to gnaw through a hazel-nut and feast on the sweet kernel inside."

" I tell you there's only enough for *me*! " said Frisky, crossly.

" But you've been eating them all day! " said Brownie. " I've watched you. Surely you've had enough? "

" Yes, I have," said Frisky. " But now I'm going to hide a lot of nuts so that when I wake up in the winter-time I can have a feast. Go away, Brownie, I'm tired of you."

" I'll make you sorry for your selfishness, Frisky," called Brownie. " You just see! "

" Pooh, how can *you* do anything to me! " said Frisky, throwing an empty nutshell at the wood-mouse and hitting him, ping, on the nose. " A little thing like you can't do *any*thing! "

But that's where Frisky was wrong. The little wood-mouse was artful, and he hid beneath a bush and watched Frisky hiding his nuts. First the squirrel put some under the leaves at the foot of the elderberry tree. Then he put a little heap in

the hollow oak tree. Then he put some under the
roots of the old beech tree not far away.

The wood-mouse watched all the hiding-places.
When Frisky had finished hiding his nuts, Brownie
ran out and stuck little twigs by them so that he
would know where they were. He didn't dare to
take the nuts whilst Frisky was still about, but he
meant to get them later on.

The days went on and week after week they grew
colder and shorter. Frisky shivered. He had a
cosy hole inside a big tree, and one day he curled

himself up there and went to sleep. He slept all the day and all the night and all the next day—and then Brownie knew that Frisky was having his long winter nap. He wouldn't wake up until a warm spell came ; perhaps not till January or February. It was quite safe for Brownie to take the nuts.

The little mouse ran to the places he had marked by the twigs. He spent all day taking the nuts one by one to his own home—a cosy little nest under the roots of a fir tree. What a crowd of nuts he had! Not one did he leave in Frisky's hiding-places!

The winter went on. Brownie stayed in his nest, half sleeping and half waking. He had plenty of nuts to nibble and he *did* enjoy them!

Then one day the sun shone warmly down and Frisky the squirrel woke up. He wriggled out of his sleeping-place and basked in the sun. How hungry he was!

"I'll go and look for my nuts!" he thought. So off he went. First he looked under the leaves

at the foot of the elderberry tree—but there
were no nuts there! Then he looked under the
roots of the beech tree—but there were none
there either! And not a single nut was to be
found in the hollow oak tree, nor in any other
place.

Frisky was puzzled and alarmed. He was dreadfully hungry. Whatever was he to do? He was
sure he wouldn't be able to go to sleep again if he
didn't get a meal.

Then his sharp ears caught the sound of a
nutshell being gnawed and he ran over to the roots
of the fir tree nearby. He knew that was where
Brownie, the wood-mouse, lived.

" Hallo! " said Brownie. " So you've woken up, have you? "

" Yes," said Frisky. " But the dreadful thing is I can't find any of my nuts. Could you give me any of yours, Brownie? "

" Did you give me any of *yours* in the autumn when I asked you? " said Brownie. " No, you didn't. You were selfish. Well, why shouldn't I be selfish, too? "

" You are quite right," said the squirrel, sadly. " I *was* selfish. I wouldn't give you any, and I had plenty. It serves me right. I cannot expect you to do what I wouldn't do. I must go without. But next year I will be generous and give to all who ask."

Brownie was not selfish really—and besides, his nuts were really those he had taken from Frisky's hiding-places. So he poked his sharp little nose out of his hole and said :

" Frisky, these are your nuts I am eating. I was cross with you when you were unkind to me, and I took your nuts. But if you see that you were wrong to treat me unkindly, then I will say that I was wrong to take your nuts. And we will share them peacefully together. What do you say to that? "

" I think you *were* wrong to take my nuts," said Frisky. " But, dear me, I was just as wrong to be selfish! So let's forgive one another and feast together, Brownie! "

Then the mouse came out of his hole under the fir tree and he and Frisky gnawed the nuts till they broke the shells and then they nibbled the kernels inside to the last crumb.

Then back went the squirrel to his sleeping-place, quite determined to share his nuts with everybody the next autumn. I expect he will too, don't you?

HUNT THE THIMBLE

ONE hot afternoon at school Miss Brown, the teacher, said the children could take their handwork into the garden to do.

"You can sit under the big chestnut tree," she said. "It will be nice and cool there."

So in great excitement the children took out their little chairs, and their work. The boys were making baskets out of cane, and the girls were sewing bags with coloured raffia. Each girl took her work and put on her thimble. Each boy took up his basket and began to weave the cane in and out. It was great fun.

Miss Brown was sitting in front of the children sewing. If any boy or girl made a mistake in their work they could run out to Miss Brown and she would show them how to put it right. First Mary ran out because she had made a wrong stitch. Then John ran out because he had taken the wrong piece of cane. Then Lucy ran out because she had lost her needle, but she soon found it again, stuck in her dress.

Belinda was sewing hard. She wanted to get her bag done in time for her mother's birthday. Her thimble was rather big for her and she had to keep pushing it down on her finger. Suddenly it fell off and rolled right away!

Belinda jumped up to get it.

" What do you want, Belinda? " asked Miss Brown.

" I've dropped my thimble," said Belinda.

" Well, hurry up and find it," said Miss Brown. " I expect it has rolled under the lilac bush behind you."

Belinda hunted for her thimble, but she couldn't see it anywhere. She crawled right under the lilac bush—and there she saw a most peculiar sight!

Two small pixies stood there, and one was
trying on a hat—and it was Belinda's thimble!
The other pixie stood looking in great delight.
The thimble made a lovely hat.

"That's my thimble!" said Belinda. At the
sound of her voice the pixies looked up, startled.
Then they ran to a little trap-door in the ground
and disappeared down it, thimble and all.

"Oh, you naughty creatures!" cried Belinda.
"You've taken my thimble and I can't get on
without it. Bring it back!"

But the pixies didn't come back. Belinda was cross. She peeped at the little trap-door, which had been left open.

" I wish I was small enough to get down there! " she said. " I'd soon get my thimble back !"

Well, no sooner had she said that than she found herself getting smaller and smaller! At last she was as small as a daisy on its stalk. She heard Miss Brown calling and calling her, but poor Belinda's voice was now so small that, of course, Miss Brown couldn't possibly hear it when she answered.

" Well, seeing that I've got my wish I think I'll go down that trap-door and get my thimble! " said Belinda. So she ran to the little trap-door and peered down it.

It was dark below, but she could just see steps going downwards. She climbed down them and found herself in a passage-way. She went along it and came to a little table set at the side. On it were burning some candles in yellow holders, and a little notice stood by one.

" Take a candle with you," was printed on the notice. Belinda thought that was a very good idea, so she picked up a candle and went on down the dark passage. She saw that she had a box of matches in the candlestick, and she was glad, for she didn't want to be left in the dark if her candle should blow out.

She went on for some way, meeting nobody at all except a large worm who most politely flattened himself out against the wall to let her pass. At last she heard excited voices in the distance, and presently she walked into a big cave, lighted by dozens of little candles, all held by pixies.

Belinda looked at them in astonishment. She had always believed in fairies, of course, but it was surprising to see so many little folk all at once.

She listened to what they were saying. One of the pixies stood on a little platform and stamped his feet. At once everyone became silent.

" Listen, pixies! " he cried. " For years we pixies have had no king because the crown has been lost. Now my friend Littlefeet, whom you

all know well, has found a marvellous silver crown.
It rolled right up to his feet this morning, and he
at once put it on his head. Well, I think that if
the silver crown came to him it means that he
ought to be our king."

Littlefeet stood up on the platform beside his
friend. In his hand he proudly held Belinda's
silver thimble. He put it on his head and bowed
to the pixies in the cave.

"It isn't a crown, it's just a hat!" shouted a
pixie loudly.

" It's just a hat! " shouted everyone.

" We don't believe it rolled up to your feet! " shouted a big pixie, standing near. " You're telling stories. You had it made for you by the goblins, and now you're pretending it's a crown so that you can be our king! "

" You're a story-teller! " shouted the pixies, angrily, and to Belinda's great alarm they swarmed up on to the platform and took hold of Littlefeet and his friend.

Littlefeet was frightened. The thimble dropped off his head and rolled away between the feet of all the pixies. Belinda couldn't see where it had gone to. She didn't have time to look for she was really feeling very worried about poor Littlefeet. The pixies were shaking him roughly, and one of them ran up with a cane to cane him.

" He deserves to be whipped for telling naughty stories! " said the pixies.

But Belinda really thought it was about time she stopped the pixies being so rough. She pushed her way to the platform and climbed up there. Then she did what Miss Brown did when she

wanted silence. She clapped her hands sharply together, and said: " CHILDREN! CHILDREN! NOT SO MUCH NOISE, PLEASE! "

In the twinkling of an eye all the pixies became silent and looked at Belinda in the greatest surprise and alarm. They did not know who she was, and they wondered how she dared to speak to them like that. They thought she must be someone very powerful indeed.

Belinda looked all round, and frowned at the pixies, just as Miss Brown did when the children had been naughty.

"What a noise!" said the little girl. "I am most surprised at you all! You have no right to shout at Littlefeet like that, and I shall certainly not let you whip him, for he doesn't deserve it."

"How do you know!" shouted a bold pixie. "Who are you, anyway?"

"Never mind who I am!" said Belinda, frowning again. "And don't speak to me like that, pixie. I can tell you exactly what happened about this silver crown. Littlefeet is not to blame."

"He had it made by the goblins!" shouted the bold pixie again.

"If you interrupt me again I shall send you out of the cave!" said Belinda, crossly. "Be quiet!"

The pixie thought he had better be quiet, and he said no more. He really thought Belinda *would* send him out of the cave!

"Now I'll tell you just what happened," said Belinda. "I and some other children were doing our handwork under the big chestnut tree, and my thimble suddenly dropped off my finger and fell on the ground. I went to get it and I crawled

under the lilac bush.   When I got under it I saw
Littlefeet trying on my silver thimble for a hat.
It had rolled to his feet, and *he* didn't know where
it had come from.   He thought it was a crown.
So I called out to him and he and his friend were
frightened and ran away.   Then I grew small and
came after them.   And here I am!   I'd like my
thimble back, so please give it to me."

The pixies listened to Belinda's story in great

surprise. They looked for the thimble and found
it. Littlefeet took it and once more put in on his
head, and all the pixies saw that it really was
nothing but a big thimble.

"It's a thimble, a thimble, a thimble!" they
cried. "Give it back to Belinda, Littlefeet."

Littlefeet was sad. He took off the thimble and
gave it to Belinda.

"Don't look so unhappy," said Belinda, kindly.
"I have an old thimble at school, and if you like
I'll give it to you to wear for a hat. Then you
will feel very grand."

"Oh, thank you!" cried the pixie. "I'll come

with you to the outside world and show you how to grow big again."

"Well, good-bye, everybody!" said Belinda to all the pixies. "Perhaps I'll see you again some day. Be good and kind to one another, and let Littlefeet wear my old thimble when I give it to him."

"Good-bye, good-bye!" cried all the little folk. Belinda went back up the long, dark passage, carrying her candle, and Littlefeet went with her. He helped her to climb out of the trapdoor underneath the lilac bush.

"Eat this," he said, pushing a little pink sweet into her hand. "It will make you big again."

Belinda ate it, and as soon as she had swallowed it she shot up to her own height again as quick as lightning. She had carried her thimble in her hand, and when she was big she slipped it on her middle finger again. Then she crawled out from beneath the bush.

"Wherever have you been, Belinda?" asked Miss Brown, crossly. "Really, anyone would think

you had been playing Hunt the Thimble, you've been so long!"

"Well," said Belinda with a laugh, "I *have* been Hunting the Thimble, Miss Brown—but I've played the game in quite a new way! Shall I tell you?"

So she told Miss Brown all that had happened, and everyone stopped work to listen to the exciting story.

"Oh, what a lucky girl you are to have such an exciting adventure!" said the other children.

"You've no idea how sweet Littlefeet looked with the thimble on his head," said Belinda. "It just fitted him beautifully. It looked like a lovely silver hat. He *was* so pleased with it."

" I wish we could give him another thimble for his own," said one of the children.

" I said I'd try and find him an old one," said Belinda. " I must look and see if I have one. Can I look in the sewing-box, Miss Brown? "

" Of course," said Miss Brown. " Go and get it."

So Belinda fetched the sewing-box and hunted about for a thimble. She felt sure her old one was there. And it was!

She took it out and tried it on her finger. " Oh dear—I really think this one would be too small for Littlefeet," she said. " I had to get a new one because it got too small for me—and as my new one only just fits him, this won't do."

" Well, look and see if there are any others the right size," said Miss Brown. " You can have any thimble that is there, if you like. I'm sure all of us would be only too pleased to give it to Littlefeet for a hat! "

I

So Belinda found one just the right size. It had a little hole at the top, so it wasn't much use as a thimble, but it didn't matter in a hat.

Belinda ran to put it under the lilac bush. " Littlefeet, Littlefeet! " she called, softly. " Here's your new hat! "

She left it there and went back to the class—and will you believe it, next day it was gone! The children hunted all round and about for it, but it certainly wasn't there.

I expect Littlefeet is wearing it proudly on his head, don't you? I wish I could see him!

BILLY THE GOAT

BILLY was a white-and-black goat who lived on the common by the roadside. He was tied to a post, but he had a good long rope, so he could wander all around and nibble at anything he liked.

One day his rope broke.

"Aha!" he said, with a bound, "I'm free! Now I can go and eat anything I like! Won't I have a good time! I'm tired of my stupid little patch of grass."

Off he went, and nobody saw him go. He ran on for some way and came to an orchard. On the

ground were many fallen apples. Billy sniffed at
them and then began to gobble them up.

Suddenly he heard an angry shout and felt a
stone hit him on the side. He looked up and saw
a man running towards him.

"Get out of the orchard!" yelled the man.
"I sell those windfall apples! How dare you eat
them! Get out!"

Billy tore off as fast as his legs would take him.
When he had left the orchard a good way behind

he slowed down because he smelt a lovely smell of cooking.

" It's over there, by that house," thought the goat. " I'll go and see."

The woman of the house had been cooking, and she had put six meat pies on the window-sill to cool. Billy trotted up to them, and it didn't take him very long to gobble up two and start on the third!

Then the woman came to the window, and wasn't she angry when she saw what Billy was doing! She ran out of the house and before Billy knew what was happening she was hitting him with a good strong walking-stick!

" I'll teach you to eat my pies! " she cried. The goat ran off bleating with pain. He was very frightened. For a long time he didn't eat even a blade of grass. Then he came to a big field, and in it were growing cabbage plants.

Billy looked all round. There was no house near.

" These must be growing wild," he thought.

" It's just a field, so perhaps these green cabbages don't belong to anyone. I'll have a nibble."

He began to eat the cabbages, but he hadn't nibbled more than two when a man rose out of the hedge nearby with a dog. When he saw Billy he was very angry.

" Get away, get away! " he shouted. " Hey, Tinker, chase that thief of a goat away! "

Tinker the dog tore across the field, and the goat was so frightened that he raced off, ran across the road and rushed into a field on the other side. Then he galloped to the far end of the field and came to a farm. He sank down trembling, but the dog had been called off and was no longer following him.

Billy stayed there for a little while. He was sad because it seemed as if he must never eat anything, and there were so many delicious things all round that a goat liked to eat! But they all belonged to other people!

A smell came to his nose and he got up to look round. It wasn't a very nice smell, but Billy didn't mind that. He liked smells of any sort. He sniffed. The smell came from a rubbish-heap over the hedge. On it the farmer's wife threw all the pieces she didn't want, and that the hens couldn't eat. Billy decided to go and have a look at it.

"Surely nobody will mind if I eat rubbish," he thought. "This has been thrown away."

So he started to scrape in the rubbish-heap— but no sooner had he begun than up rushed four fat pigs, as angry as could be!

" What are you doing? " they cried. " This is
our rubbish-heap! We root about in it, but nobody else is allowed to. Go away, you thief! "

They rushed at Billy, and he skipped aside. Off
he went at top speed, quite afraid of the four fat
pigs. He ran and ran and ran, thinking sadly that
there wasn't any place in the world that didn't
belong to *some*body. Whatever should he do?

Suddenly he stopped. Surely he knew this bit

of common? Yes—it was where he had lived so long. There was his post, and there was his broken rope! And nearby was something else! A dog, sniffing about to see what he could pick up!

Billy was very angry. He bounded up to the startled dog and butted him hard with his horns.

" Get away! " he cried. " Get away! This is *my* bit of ground! This is *my* grass! Nobody else is allowed here! "

The dog ran off, growling.

" Well, you weren't there! " he wuffed. " Your rope was broken. I thought you'd run away to find a better place."

" Every place belongs to someone," shouted the goat, " and one place is not much better than another. This is *my* place, and don't you forget it! I never in my life heard of anyone trying to take someone else's place before! "

Billy the goat lay down by his post, waiting for his master to tie him up again. He had quite forgotten that *he* had tried many other places himself that day ; he was so very angry with the dog who had come sniffing round *his* corner of the common. He wasn't going to allow *that*—no, not he!

"Well, well," said the dog, as he ran back to his kennel, "I suppose any place seems better than the one we have—till we try it. The goat can keep his bit of windy common. My old kennel for me!"

THE SKITTLES AND THE SOLDIERS

THE skittles and the wooden soldiers were always quarrelling. How they squabbled!

The soldiers said that the skittles oughtn't to live in the toy-cupboard, because they were only bits of wood, they weren't toys. The skittles said that the soldiers were only bits of wood, too, even though they did have guns over their shoulders!

The other toys got very tired of hearing them quarrel. They didn't like the soldiers very much, because they were always boasting how brave and bold they were. They didn't mind the skittles,

who were always very good-tempered when they were knocked over. But they felt very cross with both of them when they quarrelled every night.

"Look here!" said the soldiers to the skittles, "you had better live on the shelf with the bricks. You ought not to live in our cupboard with dolls, bears, and soldiers. You haven't faces or arms or legs. You're not *proper* toys. We won't have you in the toy-cupboard any more."

Well, the skittles tried to force their way into the cupboard, but it wasn't any good. The soldiers pointed their guns at them, and the skittles were afraid they might be shot. So they walked out of the cupboard and arranged themselves on the low shelf where the boxes of bricks were kept. They were very cross.

Now that night, when it was dark, who should come into the nursery but Green-Eyes the cat! She had come to see what mischief she could do, for she was jealous of the toys. Peggy and Annie so often played with them when she wanted them to play with *her*.

She stalked into the room.

" Sh-sh-sh-sh-sh! " whispered the toys. " Here's that horrid cat! Be careful, toys! "

Most of them were safely in the toy-cupboard— but Bruiny, the little brown bear, had been left in Peggy's chair. How afraid he was when he saw the cat! He jumped down from the chair and ran towards the toy-cupboard as fast as his fat little legs would carry him.

Puss saw him. Her green eyes flashed with delight. Here was a toy bear to tease!

She pounced on him and he fell to the floor calling for help in his little grunty voice. The toys looked at one another in dismay.

"Who will help Bruiny? Who will save him from that cat?"

The golliwog wouldn't. He was scared of the cat's sharp claws. The big doll wouldn't. She didn't want to get her dress torn. The woolly lamb wouldn't. He was too small. The white duck wouldn't. She was too frightened even to quack.

"What about the bold, brave soldiers?" cried

the golliwog suddenly. "They will fight the cat!
They are always saying how brave they are."

"Yes, soldiers, go and save Bruiny from the
cat!" cried the doll, and all the toys joined in.

But oh, those soldiers! They took one peep at
that big green-eyed cat and they shook and shivered from top to toe!

They tiptoed to the very back of the cupboard
and there they stood, not saying a word!

"Help, help!" cried Bruiny. "The cat is
scratching me! Help, before she eats me!"

All the toys were worried to hear poor Bruiny
calling like that. They pushed the soldiers to the
front of the cupboard and commanded them to go
and save Bruiny. But no, the soldiers wouldn't
stir an inch, not an inch! They were much too
scared!

Poor Bruiny! Would nobody save him? Just
as the little woolly lamb was trying to make up
his mind that *he* would go and help him, the
skittles on the shelf came alive!

Yes, they had heard Bruiny's cries, and although

they were only skittles, they were brave and kind. *They* didn't mind if they were hurt or not—weren't they made to be knocked down? They would go and save poor little Bruiny.

They grew two skinny arms each, and a big foot grew at the bottom of their single legs. And off the shelf they hopped, all the nine skittles waving their thin arms about and making a curious squeaking noise.

They hopped to where the cat was teasing Bruiny, and surrounded Green-Eyes. The cat looked at them in surprise, and then put out her paw and knocked a skittle down. It fell over with a bang, but to the cat's great surprise it jumped up again and ran up beneath her nose. Punch! The skittle hit the puss on the nose and made her blink!

Then all the skittles joined in the fight. Crack! Punch! Blip! Smack! How they went for that astonished puss! They smacked her nose, they trod on her tail, they punched her paws, and they didn't seem to mind falling down in the least.

Puss lashed out with her paw and every single

one of the skittles fell over and rolled about. The cat was pleased. Ha! that would teach those silly skittles not to meddle with *her*! But up they jumped again, and dear me, how they pummelled her from nose to tail! There were so many of them that even if she knocked down four or five there seemed just as many left!

Bruiny slipped away. He was scratched and frightened, but not much hurt. He hurried to the toy-cupboard and sat down to get his breath.

" Oh, those brave skittles! " he said. " Look

at them! Did you ever see anyone so bold as they are! They don't mind that cat a bit! Why didn't the soldiers save me? They always tell us how brave they are!"

"They were afraid," said the woolly lamb in his little bleating voice. "Ho, ho, they were afraid!"

The soldiers stood quite still. They didn't dare to say a word, they were so ashamed of themselves. The big doll pushed open the door of the toy-cupboard so that all the toys might see the great fight that was going on. The soldiers didn't want to see it, but the toys turned them so that they had to watch.

Those skittles were enjoying themselves! Although Bruiny had escaped, that didn't matter. The skittles were going to spank that cat until she was sorry she had ever come into the nursery! Bump! Bang! The skittles fell over time and again, but up they jumped as plucky as ever!

The cat became scared at last. She thought she would go to the kitchen. She turned tail and ran for the door.   After her went the skittles with a hop, skip and a jump, for they had no more than one leg each.   They gave the naughty cat a parting smack and then hopped back to their shelf, warm and happy.

But the toys were not going to allow them to live on the shelf with the bricks.   Oh no, they were better than the soldiers, they must certainly live in the toy-cupboard!

" You must live with us again, skittles! " cried the big doll.   " You are brave and bold, good and kind.   The soldiers are poor things—they couldn't even go out to help poor Bruiny!   *They*

shall live on the cold shelf outside. *You* shall live here with us, and we will be proud of you always!"

The skittles hopped over to the cupboard, and what a fuss the toys made of them! As for the soldiers the golliwog made them march out of the cupboard in a straight line, and to the shelf they had to go.

They arranged themselves there in a row—and

how surprised Annie and Peggy were in the morning!

" Who put the soldiers on the shelf? " said Annie.

" And who put the skittles in the corner of the
cupboard where the soldiers live? " wondered
Peggy. The golliwog gave a funny sort of squeak,
and the children looked at him.

" I'm sure you could tell us why, if only you
could speak to us! " said Annie. " Do tell us,
Golly! "

But alas! Golly couldn't, although he tried
hard. Wouldn't Peggy and Annie have liked to
know all that happened in the night!

THE TWISTY GNOME'S STOCKINGS

ONCE upon a time there lived a sly-looking gnome just outside Diddle Village. He used to go about with a barrowful of flowers, selling them, and then one day it was found that he stole into the Prince of Dreamland's lovely garden each night, and took the flowers growing there! So, of course, he was punished, and not allowed to sell flowers any more.

Now the only other thing he could do was to knit. You should have seen him knit! His four needles went so fast that you could hardly see them! He knitted stockings, so he had to have four needles. He didn't knit anything else. His wife helped him, and between them they knitted enough to stock a shop.

That's why they started a stocking-shop. Mrs. Twisty cleared the front room of her cottage and in the window she put two shelves. On the shelves she draped the stockings she and Twisty had knitted. They really were beautiful stockings. They were all colours—blue, red, yellow, pink, purple, green—and some of them were striped.

The little folk of Diddle Village liked the look of them very much, and although they thought the Twisty Gnome a horrid fellow, they bought his stockings because they were quite the best in the place.

The Twisty Gnome and his wife couldn't make enough! They sold their stockings cheaply, and at the end of every week their shop was empty. They were always knitting!

Twisty got quite tired of it.

" I wish I need never knit another stocking in

my life!" he said. "I'm tired of wool and needles!"

"I wouldn't mind if we could sell them for more money," said Mrs. Twisty, knitting busily. "But the little folk wouldn't buy them if they were dearer."

Twisty knitted fast and thought hard. Then an idea came into his wicked little mind and he smiled. He put down his knitting and sidled up to his wife. He whispered to her what he had thought of, and she was pleased.

"Sh!" she said, looking round. "Don't let anyone hear you! You can start to-night!"

So that night Twisty set out in the darkness. In his pocket he had a note of all the people who had bought new stockings from him that day. He stole to Mrs. Tubby's first. He peeped in at the window. Mrs. Tubby was in bed, and a candle was burning by her side. Twisty saw that the pair of fine new red stockings he had sold her were hanging over the bedrail. Mrs. Tubby blew the candle out and settled down into bed. When she began to snore gently Twisty put his hand in at the window and took the stockings!

Then he went to Mister Curly's, but the window was tight shut there. So he went to Dame Twinkle's and, what luck, found her stockings hanging outside on the line!

Then he went to Elf Tiptoe's. She slept in a hole in a tree, so it was quite easy to steal her neatly-folded new stockings and pop them into his bag.

Twisty went home with five pairs of stockings that night. He mixed them up with the ones in the window and went to bed.

In the morning, just what he expected to happen, *did* happen! Along came Mrs. Tubby, complaining that her stockings had been stolen in the night, so she must have a new pair.

" I don't expect you've got another pair of *red* stockings! " she said.

" Yes, it so happens I have! " said Twisty, and he took from the window the very stockings he had stolen from her the night before!

" Oh, good! " said Mrs. Tubby, pleased. She had no idea they were really her own stockings!

" I'm so sorry you had them stolen," said the Twisty Gnome, cunningly. " But see, Mrs. Tubby, I'm a kind-hearted fellow—I'll only charge you half-price this time, because I'm so sorry for you! "

" Well, well! " said Mrs. Tubby, delighted. " Of all the nice, generous gnomes! And I'd always thought you such a mean, dishonest fellow. Thank you very much, Twisty."

One by one came all the others whose stockings had been stolen, and each of them was delighted to find that Twisty would only charge them half-price. Soon the word went round that Twisty was a fine generous fellow, and he was pleased.

About every fourth night the cunning gnome went out stealing the stockings he had sold. He began to make a great deal of money, for, you see, he sold each pair twice over, and although he only charged half-price the second time, it was enough to fill his purse to overflowing!

The folk of Diddle Village were puzzled to know who was stealing their stockings.

" Is it a big centipede? " they wondered. " A centipede has a hundred legs, so he needs a lot of stockings."

But nobody knew : and Twisty was much too wily to be caught stealing.

Now one day he sold a pair of yellow stockings to Dame Waddle. She was proud of them and put them on the very same day to walk over to her sister's. She had a nail in her shoe, and when she took off her stockings that night she discovered that the nail had torn a little hole underneath the foot of one of her beautiful new stockings.

She was a tidy person, so she thought she would mend the hole before she went to bed—but dear me, she hadn't any yellow wool—only a little piece of orange wool in her work-basket.

" Well, I'll mend it with that and then tomorrow I'll buy some yellow wool, undo the mend and darn the hole properly," she thought.   So she carefully mended the hole with the orange wool, then laid the stockings over the bed-rail by the window.

That night they were stolen, so, in great distress, Dame Waddle went to Twisty's shop again to ask for another pair, this time at half-price.

" Well, you're lucky," said the gnome, looking through his stock. " I've got a pair for you, about the same colour as those I sold you before."

Dame Waddle was pleased. She took them away in a parcel, and when she got home she undid them—and dear me, she suddenly caught sight of a very neat little orange darn in the foot of one stocking! She sat and stared and stared at it—

and then her face grew red with anger. She guessed what Twisty had been doing!

" The mean, wicked gnome! " she frowned. " So that's what he's done—stolen the stockings he has sold, and then sold them again to the same people he stole them from! My, my, he's a wicked fellow! "

She went straight to Mister Grandy, the head brownie of the village, and told him what she knew. And Mister Grandy set a trap for Twisty. He went to Twisty's shop and bought a pair of blue stockings. He put them over a chair near his window that night, and then got into bed and pretended to snore. But outside, hidden in the bushes, were four of the brownies of Diddle Village, watching!

Along crept Twisty as usual—and just as he had got hold of the stockings through the window somebody got hold of *him*! He was caught! He wriggled and struggled, but it was no use. The four brownies had got him, and Mister Grandy jumped out of bed and gave a hand, too.

He was well spanked by everyone whose stockings he had stolen—and now he and Mrs. Twisty have to make the stockings for the whole of Diddle Village at a penny a pair! They are as poor as church mice, and they will never be rich—but that's their own fault, isn't it?

THE BOLD GOLLIWOG

THERE was once a bold and boastful golliwog who thought the world of himself. The other toys got very tired of him, and one night they told him they were very glad there was only one golly in the nursery—they simply didn't know what they would do, if there were two!

"Ho!" said the golliwog, in a very nasty voice. "So, that's what you think, is it? Well, let me tell you I'm very tired of your company. I never knew such a silly fellow as the teddy bear, for instance. And as for the three dolls, why, I'd rather talk to a beetle than listen to their foolish chatter! "

" You horrid fellow! " cried the three dolls, almost in tears. " Go and find a beetle to talk to then! He would be fit company for you! "

" I shall *not* go to find a beetle," said the golliwog, haughtily. " I don't want to make friends with beetles. But I shall go out alone this very night and look for another GOLLIWOG! Yes, and I'll bring him back with me, too, and then he and I will be friends and we needn't take any notice of you soldiers and stuffed animals and chattering dolls! Ha, what do you think of that? "

" What, go out alone at night! " cried the bear, in alarm. " You must be mad! No toy is supposed to wander about alone outside."

" Pooh! I'M not afraid," said the golliwog. " Anyway, I'm going, this very night. You wait and see! "

Sure enough, at twelve o'clock, when the house was dark and quiet, the golliwog started off by himself, without even saying good-bye to the other toys. He climbed out of the window and jumped down into the garden. He felt very bold indeed, and was quite sure he would be able to bring back another golliwog with him for company in the nursery.

He went down the garden path—but just round the corner he bumped into something very sharp and prickly.

" Ooh! " he cried, in alarm. " What's that? "

" It's me, Prickles, the hedgehog," said a cross voice. " Why don't you look where you're going? "

" Why don't *you*? " said the golliwog, sharply.

" Because I don't need to," said the hedgehog, with a giggle. " I don't get hurt if I run into people—it's the silly fellows who run into *me* that get hurt! Watch! "

To the golliwog's dismay the hedgehog suddenly ran right into him, and my goodness me, he pricked the golliwog all down his leg and made him howl in pain. On went the hedgehog up the path, chuckling loudly to himself.

"Ill-mannered creature!" shouted the golliwog loudly, and turned angrily to go on his way—but the very next moment he trod on a slippery worm and fell flat on his nose! He got up and rubbed his dirty face.

"How dare you tread on me, you clumsy creature!" said the worm crossly. "Let me pass at once."

The golliwog stepped back—and trod on another worm just behind him. Down he went again, this time on his back, but by the time he was sitting

up and getting back his breath, the worms had disappeared into their holes.

Then, gracious goodness, a strange noise sounded just above his head, and something caught hold of him with sharp claws! The golliwog screamed in fright.

"Too-whoo, too-whoo!" said the loud voice. It was an owl that had seen the golliwog move, and had thought he was a mouse! So he had swooped down and caught him in his sharp talons.

"What are you?" said the owl, in disgust, when he found that the golliwog wasn't a mouse.

" I'm a golliwog," said the toy. " Let me go."

" Are you good to eat? " asked the owl.

" No, not a bit," said the golliwog, hurriedly. " If anyone ate me, they would have a most dreadful tummy-ache."

The owl let him go.

" What are you wandering about at night for? " he asked. " Don't you know that all good toys and children are in bed and asleep? "

" I'm looking for another golliwog like me," said the golliwog.

The owl laughed. " Hoo, hoo, hoo! You won't find another creature as ugly as you anywhere, I'm sure of that! You're the only creature I've seen that's so black. Why don't you wash your face? "

The golliwog was so offended that he walked away without saying another word. He was very angry indeed, and I shouldn't like to tell you of all the things he thought about that owl.

He stepped on something soft that at once rose high in the air and made the golliwog cry out in fright. It was a frog!

" Careless, clumsy creature! " cried the frog, angrily. " You stepped on my foot! Be careful or I will tell the big white duck to eat you! Go and wash your dirty face! "

The golliwog was most offended again. He hated to be told that his face wanted washing, for he knew perfectly well that it was clean, although it was black.

He stalked on, wondering what in the wide world would happen next, and hoping and hoping he would soon find another golliwog to walk with —for he was really feeling rather frightened!

He was also cold, for the night was chilly. As he stumbled along in the dark he came up against something soft and warm. It was big, and the golliwog didn't know what it was. He sat down beside it to get warm himself—and as he snuggled into the warm soft thing, it moved. Then a big mouth came round to him and picked him up in its teeth!

It was a goat, lying down in a field, half asleep. Now, as you know, goats will eat anything from a

newspaper to a piece of wire, and this goat was
quite ready to nibble a nice, soft golliwog!

"Oh! Oh! Let me go!" cried the golliwog,
struggling hard. The goat nipped him with his
teeth, and the golliwog stopped wriggling.

"I'm only a golliwog!" wept the toy. "Only
a poor little golliwog, lost and frightened. Oh, I
want to go back to the nursery! Oh, let me go,
kind animal, whatever you are!"

The goat put him down. He had had a very

good meal that evening and he really didn't feel hungry. But all the same he didn't mean to let the golliwog go. No, he would do nicely for a bit of breakfast in the morning! So he put his hairy chin on the frightened toy and then shut his eyes to go to sleep again.

When the golliwog heard the goat breathing gently and evenly, and knew he was asleep, he wriggled carefully away. He slipped a big stone under the goat's chin to make him think he was still resting on the golliwog, and then off he ran.

How he ran! Through the hedge and up the garden path to the nursery as if a thousand goats, owls and frogs were after him! He climbed in through the window and flung himself down on the floor, panting.

" What's the matter, what's the matter? " asked the toys, crowding round him.

The golliwog got back his breath and sat up. He went as red as his black face would let him, and then he spoke in a humble little voice.

" I've had a lesson," he said. " I've learnt

that I'm not so grand and wonderful as I thought
I was. I couldn't find another golliwog—and dear
me, the creatures I met outside to-night weren't
nearly as nice as you, dolls, soldiers and animals!
So I've come back to say I'm sorry, and please will
you forgive me, and let me be friends again? "

Well, the toys were glad to see him safe back, for
they were very kind-hearted. So, of course, they
forgave the golliwog, and he doesn't brag or boast
any more. But they really can't help smiling
when they think of his adventures—especially of
the slippery worms he fell over. I can't help
smiling either, can you?

GROWN-UP WILLIAM

THERE was once a little boy who thought himself very grown-up. His name was William, but his mother called him Billy for short.

William didn't like that.

" Please call me William," he said. " It's more grown up. I think Billy sounds silly."

So everyone called him William, and he was very pleased with himself.

One day he asked his mother if he could go to the farm and fetch the eggs. Mary the maid usually fetched them every day, but she was busy ironing, so William thought he would like to fetch them.

" But, William dear, it's quite a long way, and the fields are muddy and wet," said his mother. " You're not very careful where you walk, you know—and besides, you've got your best suit on to-day, while your other is being washed. No, William dear, you can't go."

" Mother, do you think I can't walk through the fields without dirtying my shoes! " cried William, quite annoyed. " I'm quite grown-up enough to go to the farm, even in my best clothes. You know you can trust me not to dirty them and tear them like the other silly boys."

" I can't help it, William," said his mother. " I don't want you to go. You're not old enough, even though you think yourself so very grown-up. You're only a little boy really, you know, and little boys must do what they are told."

William was as cross as could be. He knew that all the children would be coming out of school, and he did so badly want them to see him in his best suit, walking through the muddy fields all by himself to fetch the eggs from the farm. Not even Harry, the big boy next door, was allowed to go through the fields in the muddy weather, because he came back so dirty.

Well, the more William thought of it, the more he wanted to go. And at last he thought he would just show his mother how clever he was. He would take the basket and go for the eggs without telling anyone! Then, when he came back with them, all nice and clean still in his best suit, how pleased and proud everyone would be!

He took the egg-basket and set off, creeping quietly out of the back gate. He went down the lane and climbed carefully over the stile that led across the fields. How slowly he walked, taking care to choose all the driest places!

At last he reached the farm. The farmer's wife was most surprised to see him all alone.

" My, you are growing up, to come across our muddy fields all alone! " she said. " You're getting quite a man! "

William was so pleased with himself. He said good afternoon most politely and set off home again with the eggs in the basket. There were eighteen of them, so they felt quite heavy.

" The children will just be coming out of school when I climb over the stile into the lane," he thought to himself. " I shall pretend not to notice them, I'll be so careful where I walk that my eyes will be on the ground all the time. How grand the children will think me! "

But dear me, just as he was crossing the last muddy field, what should come towards him but a troop of big cackling geese! They were on their way to the stream, but William didn't know that. He thought they were going to peck him, and he was terribly frightened.

"Hisss-sss-sss-sss!" said the geese, going right up to William. William screamed and ran away. He didn't look where he was going and fell flat into the muddy ditch! Oh my! What a mess he was in! He was covered with mud from head

to foot, and you couldn't tell which was his face and which wasn't, it was so splashed with mud.

The eggs fell to the ground and smashed. Poor William! He got up and ran shrieking to the stile. All the school children were passing by and they stopped to look at William in astonishment.

"Poor William!" said Harry, the big boy from next door. "The geese have frightened him! He's only a little boy, so no wonder he was afraid. Come on, William, I'll take you home!"

Weeping big tears, poor William was taken home by Harry, and his mother couldn't believe her eyes when she saw him.

"Where *have* you been!" she cried. "And oh, William, your best suit is all spoilt!"

William flew to her arms and sobbed out all his story. How ashamed he was! And what a little boy he felt, not a bit grown-up at all!

"Poor Billy!" said his kind mother, hugging him. "You're not a very big boy yet, are you? You're only my little Billy who's frightened of the silly geese! Well, dear, you've no more clothes to wear, so you'll have to go to bed whilst I wash all the mud off these."

So Billy went to bed for the rest of the day. He didn't grumble because he knew he deserved a punishment, and his mother had comforted him when she might have scolded.

" I shan't be William any more," he thought. " I'm not big enough. I'll be Billy and I'll do as I'm told."

So now he's Billy—and to tell the truth, people like Billy ever so much more than they liked that stuck-up little William!

THE DARING CLOWN

THE toy-cupboard was very full. Peter and Biddy had so many toys that it was really quite difficult to get them all into the cupboard. They had four uncles and six aunts, so, you see, they were always having presents.

They had dolls, golliwogs, bears, rabbits, balls, skittles, cats, dogs, books, trains, and heaps of other things besides. They had a wheelbarrow, a big box of coloured bricks, a spade and pail each and a box of big glass beads. And the last things of all, given to them that very morning, were most exciting—a clown that could go head over heels when he was wound up, and a motor-car that would run ever such a long way.

There was no room in the toy cupboard for the clown and the motor-car, so when they went to bed that night Peter and Biddy stood them just outside the cupboard door.

The toys came alive as soon as the house was quiet. They crowded round the new car and were most excited to see the new clown. He went head over heels twelve times to show them

how clever he was. They thought he was wonderful.

"How does the motor-car go?" asked the curly-haired doll. "Is this the key to wind it up?"

"*I'll* show you how to do it!" said the clown grandly. "I watched Peter winding it this morning."

He wound up the car, and then, goodness me, he got into it! It wouldn't go until the brake was taken off—it was just like a real car—and the clown was just going to take off the brake when the biggest golliwog stopped him.

"No, no," he said. "You mustn't drive this car. It's Peter's. You might have an accident."

"Pooh!" said the clown, making a rude face at the golliwog. "I'm too clever to have an accident! I tell you I can drive this car perfectly well! You just see! I'll go all round the nursery and back again!"

"But you really mustn't!" said all the toys together. "It's naughty of you. Suppose you broke the car! Whatever would Peter say?"

" I don't care! " said the daring clown. He took off the brake and the car shot forward. Round the nursery it went, and the clown waved his hand to the frightened toys. But goodness me, when the car came near the nursery door, it saw that it was open, and it ran straight out of it!

The toys cried out in alarm, and ran to the door. They saw the clown clinging to the steering-wheel, looking very much afraid. The car shot on down the passage and came to the garden door, which Daddy had forgotten to close that night. So out into the garden ran the clockwork car, and rushed down the path.

The toys clung to one another in fright. What a dreadful thing to happen! They felt quite sure that there would be a dreadful accident. And even as they thought that, they heard a terrible, smashing, crashing noise, and the clown's voice reached them, shouting in fear : " Help! Help! "

The toys ran down the passage and out into the garden. Then they saw the accident. The car had run straight into a very large hedgehog and had turned upside down!

The clown had been thrown out on top of the prickly hedgehog, and there he had stuck, all the prickles sticking into him! He was shouting in pain, and the hedgehog, just as much alarmed as everybody else, was trying to shake him off his back.

The toys ran to the rescue. They dragged the daring clown off the hedgehog's back, and he sat on the ground, groaning and moaning. The hedge-hog scuttled off at once and disappeared through the hedge, making up his mind never to go into *that* garden again.

The toys turned the car the right way up, and then, oh dear, they found that one of the wheels was off and the brake was bent almost in two. They *were* upset!

" What are we going to do about it? " asked the biggest golliwog. " The car is broken."

" What are you going to do about *me*? " cried the clown. " Never mind the silly old car. I'm hurt! I can't turn somersaults any more! "

" Well, it serves you right," said the curly-haired doll crossly. " You *would* go in the car, and we told you not to. Golliwog, how are we going to get the clown and the car back to the nursery."

The brown bear had a good idea.

"What about the wheelbarrow?" he said. "Shall we fetch that and put the clown and the car in it? Then I can wheel them both back. I'm stronger than any of you, and it won't take long to get both toys into the house."

"I *won't* ride in a wheelbarrow!" cried the clown angrily. "I should look silly."

"Well, you'll look just what you *are*, then," said the sailor doll smartly. "You *are* silly! You've given us all a lot of trouble by being so daring."

The bear fetched the wheelbarrow and the toys

lifted in the clown and the clockwork car. Then the bear carefully wheeled them into the nursery. The clown hated it, because he knew he looked silly, sitting in the barrow—and he had felt so grand when he had shot off in the motor-car!

"Now we must mend the motor-car," said the sailor doll. "It would never do for Peter and Biddy to find it broken in the morning."

"Will you mend me too?" asked the clown. "I can't go head over heels now. I am much more important than the motor-car."

"No, you're not," said the toys. "You're just a silly, bad-mannered clown, who can't even say he's sorry for causing so much trouble. You're the newest toy here, and you should have been humble to us, instead of showing off like that. We think it serves you right to have an accident, and unless you try to make yourself a much nicer clown, we shan't like you at all."

The clown wouldn't say he was sorry. He just sat and sulked and the toys took no more notice of him. They set to work to mend the car. The sailor doll put the wheel on again and the biggest golliwog bent the brake straight. Then the toys looked all over the car to see if there was anything else wrong, but there wasn't. It seemed quite all right.

When morning came Biddy and Peter ran into the nursery to play with their new toys. The motor-car went quite all right—but, of course, the clown couldn't turn head over heels!

"He's no use!" said Peter. "He's gone wrong already. We'll give him to Cook's little boy. He will love to have him for a doll."

So that was what happened to the daring clown. He was taken away and the toys never saw him again.

"We'd have mended him if he'd been nice," said the toys. "But he wasn't. So it serves him right."

And it did, didn't it?

THE GOBLIN IN THE BOX

THE Wise Man, Mister Hush-Hush, had a goblin in a box, who did everything he was commanded. Hush-hush had only to tap the box and say: " Come out, goblin, and do this," or " do that," and at once the box would fly open. Out would come the ugly little goblin, grow to full size in a twink, and obey his master at once.

Hush-hush had a servant to look after his house. This was Slip-Shod, a lazy and untidy brownie. Slip-Shod often watched his master tapping the goblin-box, and how he wished he had a goblin to do his bidding too!

Now one day Mister Hush-Hush went out for the day, and before he left the house he called Slip-Shod to him and gave him his orders.

" There are no meals to cook to-day," he said. " So you can do a bit of gardening. Dig over that bed just at the back of the house—and do it properly, or I'll know the reason why when I come back! "

Hush-Hush went out. Slip-Shod finished his housework, and then ate his dinner. Then he looked out of the window. It was a very hot, sunny day. Slip-Shod sighed when he thought of the digging he had to do. If there was one thing he really did hate, it was digging. You *had* to work hard at digging—you couldn't help it.

Then a naughty thought came into Slip-Shod's mind. He would get the goblin in the box to do the digging for him! It would all be done before Hush-Hush came back, then, and nobody would ever know! So he crept into the Wise Man's study and looked round for the little red box where the goblin lived.

Slip-Shod picked up the box and took it into the kitchen. Then he tapped on it, and tried to speak in his master's deep voice.

" Come out, goblin, and dig over the bed at the back of the house! "

The lid flicked open and out jumped the ugly goblin. In a trice he was full-size, bigger than Slip-Shod, and he stared in anger and surprise when he saw that it was the little brownie who had commanded him to come out and not his master. But he had to do what he was commanded. so he set off.

Slip-Shod rubbed his hands in glee. What a good idea of his! Now he could go upstairs and lie down for a sleep on his bed, whilst the goblin did his work. He looked out of the window. Yes, the goblin had found a spade and was beginning to dig.

Slip-Shod didn't much like the look on the goblin's face. It was most strange—almost as if he were going to enjoy himself very much—and yet he really must be *very* cross! Well, well, Slip-

Shod didn't care what the goblin looked like or felt—*he* was going to have a nice, cosy nap!

Upstairs he went and in a few minutes he was snoring hard. He didn't wake up until two hours later. He jumped up quickly, for he was expecting the Wise Man back soon after tea, and he wanted to get the goblin into the box again.

He looked out of the window to see how the goblin was getting on—and, oh, my goodness me, he found himself looking down into the most enormous hole he had ever seen! The goblin had dug and dug and dug, using his magic strength

with all his might—and he had made the most
enormous hole you ever saw, just at the back of
the house. It really looked as if at any moment
the house would topple into it! The goblin had
piled up the earth from the hole at the end of the
garden, and it had made a big hill, as high as the
hole was deep! What a sight it was, to be sure!

Slip-Shod flew downstairs, and out into the
garden. Right down at the bottom of the hole

the goblin was still working. A shovelful of earth caught Slip-Shod in the face and he choked.

"Hie, goblin, stop, stop!" he roared. "The house will fall into the hole! Stop, I say!"

"I only stop for my master, not for you!" shouted back the goblin. "If the house falls in, it will be your fault! Look, it's rocking a bit now!"

To Slip-Shod's horror the house certainly was rocking. He gave a cry of terror and rushed round to the front. He leaned over the gate to see if Hush-Hush was coming home—and to his great relief he saw his master walking up the road!

Slip-Shod ran to meet him, shouting at the top of his voice. "Master! Master! The house is falling into a hole! Come before it's too late."

In the greatest astonishment Hush-Hush ran to his house—only just in time, for it was about to tumble into the gaping hole just beside it. Hush-Hush guessed in a moment what had happened, and he called sternly to the goblin.

"Come out! Put the house farther off, or it will fall into the hole. Then go back to your box!"

The goblin shot out of the hole in a hurry, for he was afraid of the Wise Man. He gave the house a great push and it immediately moved three feet away from the hole, so that now there was no danger of it falling.

Then the goblin made a rude face at Slip-Shod and jumped back into his little red box. The lid flicked down and he was safe.

Hush-Hush turned to the trembling Slip-Shod.

" Lazy, deceitful brownie! " he said angrily. " Fill up this enormous hole at once! "

" F-f-f-f-f-fill up this h-h-h-hole! " stammered Slip-Shod in horror. " Why, it would take me years, master! "

" That doesn't matter," said Hush-Hush. " You caused the hole to be dug, and you can just fill it up. A little hard work will do you good."

Slip-Shod is still filling up the hole. Goodness knows when he will have finished! It's taken him four years already! Poor, silly Slip-Shod!

PRINTED IN GREAT BRITAIN BY ROBERT MACLEHOSE AND CO LTD.
THE UNIVERSITY PRESS, GLASGOW